GLOBAL AFRICAN VOICES
Dominic Thomas, editor

THE PAST AHEAD

A NOVEL

GILBERT GATORE

TRANSLATED BY
MARJOLIJN DE JAGER

FRENCH
VOICES

INDIANA UNIVERSITY PRESS
Bloomington and Indianapolis

This book is a publication of

Indiana University Press
601 North Morton Street
Bloomington, Indiana 47404-3797 USA

iupress.indiana.edu

Telephone orders   800-842-6796
Fax orders   812-855-7931

This work, published as part of a program providing publication assistance, received financial support from the French Ministry of Foreign Affairs, the Cultural Services of the French Embassy in the United States, and FACE (French American Cultural Exchange).

Manufactured in the United States of America

Library of Congress Cataloging-in-Publication Data

Gatore, Gilbert, [date]
 [Passé devant soi. English]
 The past ahead : a novel / Gilbert Gatore ; translated by Marjolijn de Jager.
  p. cm. — (Global African voices)
 Includes bibliographical references.
 ISBN 978-0-253-00665-3 (cl : alk. paper) — ISBN 978-0-253-00666-0 (pb : alk. paper)
ISBN 978-0-253-00950-0 (eb)
 I. De Jager, Marjolijn. II. Title.
 PQ2707.A86P3713 2012
 843′.92—dc23

2012015756

1 2 3 4 5   17 16 15 14 13 12

To my parents,
to Pierre and Maddy Le Bas,

thank you.

I have broken an order, and
the guilty are never bored.
—J.-M. COETZEE, *IN THE HEART OF THIS LAND*

What better is there to be done when
there's no doubt whatsoever that it's too late?

ACKNOWLEDGMENTS

The translator wishes to express her sincere gratitude to Dee Mortensen, senior editor at Indiana University Press, and to Dominic Thomas, professor of French & Francophone studies at University of California, Los Angeles, for their unswerving encouragement and support for the translation of Gilbert Gatore's novel. Without such enthusiasm for and faith in the importance of francophone African literature, works such as these would remain unknown to the large audience that is waiting to discover these voices.

I am equally grateful to the French Embassy's program of French Voices, which has supported this publication with the generosity of its funding.

And, as always, warm gratitude goes to David Vita, my first and acutely critical reader, without whose daily presence and support my work would be much more difficult.

INTRODUCTION

While working on the translation of Gilbert Gatore's novel, I kept asking myself two questions. First, why had he written this particular novel? It is a story in which Niko, one of the two protagonists, is developed in such a way that the reader comes to have great empathy for him, feeling increasing compassion for Niko and even anger with those around him, since all but one of the villagers cast him aside. Then, when we learn much later in the novel that Niko is also the perpetrator of horrendous crimes, I wondered how, despite the horror of his character's actions, the author had made it possible for me to continue feeling some sort of compassion for him. The answer came just recently when in an interview on *Art Beat*[1] the author and journalist Roger Rosenblatt was asked why writers write. He gave four reasons: "to make suffering endurable, evil intelligible, justice desirable, and love possible." Whether Gilbert Gatore would agree with this response I cannot and do not know, but for me, his reader, he has succeeded on all four fronts.

Phébus, his French publisher, provides us with the following biographical information: "Gilbert Gatore was born in Rwanda in 1981. On the eve of the civil war, his father gave him *The Diary of Anne Frank* to read. Profoundly moved, the young boy decided, like the heroine, to keep a diary throughout the conflict. When he fled the country with his family in 1997, Zairian customs officers took everything they had, including the precious notebooks. Ever since, he has tried to recover the strength and truth of those emotions in his writing." By keeping a diary, suffering was made en-

durable both for Anne Frank and, generations later, for Gilbert Gatore. (On a personal level, for a woman whose origin is Dutch and
who herself has rather vivid childhood memories of World War II,
it is particularly moving to learn that Gatore's earliest inspiration
came from Anne Frank.)

The novel's two characters, Isaro and Niko, are mirror images
of one another, even though at first they appear to be each other's
most extreme opposites: a beautiful, talented, smart young woman,
raised with all the comforts of a middle class family, and an ugly,
handicapped, ostracized young man, victim and executioner, self-
seeker and self-concealer. Everything each of them embodies is
wholly lacking in the other. However, as the story progresses it becomes clear that they are two sides of what is essentially the same
person, especially as we realize that it is also a novel within a novel,
since Niko is the protagonist in the tale that Isaro is in the process of writing. Gatore has explained in an on-line interview that
"the contrast is . . . inside themselves as well as between the two
characters; . . . Isaro is the reverse of Niko" (le contraste . . . est à
l'intérieur d'eux-mêmes et entre les deux personnages; . . . Isaro est
la renversée de Niko).[2]

Although Niko is "voicing the perpetrator's perspective,"[3] it
is very different from the speech of Jean Hatzfeld's real-life crimi-
nals. The latter remain incomprehensible to the listener. Although,
as the French historian Gérard Prunier wrote about the genocide in
Rwanda, "Understanding why they died is the best and most fitting
memorial we can raise for the victims. Letting their deaths go un-
recorded, or distorted by propaganda, or misunderstood through
simple clichés, would in fact bring the last touch to the killers' work
in completing the victims' dehumanization."[4]

Niko, the fictional perpetrator, allows us to begin to find evil
intelligible, no matter with how much hesitation and distaste we
do so. By the time we discover what he has done once an adult, we
know all about his wretched, motherless, and loveless childhood,
we have come to care about him, and we know that he despises
himself enough to vanish from society—and by so doing he begins to make evil intelligible for us. It is just one case, but it is an
extremely compelling one.

"Write about what you want to know," Rosenblatt says, and so Isaro does. But it is too late for her. She seeks to understand evil by writing Niko's story. In *Women Witnessing Terror*,[5] Anne Cubilie outlines that the vocation of "giving testimony is about being a witness to impossible storytelling, and also a performative act between the mute witnesses, the dead, the survivor witness and the witness to the survivor." Trying to verbalize what in essence cannot be spoken is, indeed, impossible storytelling. Yet merely *attempting* to convey what is incomprehensible might be a way to survive tragedy. It is this urgency that leads Isaro to abandon her studies in Paris, leave France, and undertake a research project that entails interviewing perpetrators in her homeland while at the same time working on her own imaginary story of Niko. He is in a sense the witness to the survivor she has been so far, but, in her case, creating the monster who is the very embodiment of evil is not sufficient to keep her going. And it doesn't. It cannot help her in her attempt to be part of a community again or to live an ordinary, everyday life. She realizes that justice is, indeed, desirable, but she is unable to find it anywhere or to help it materialize.

Finally, and only briefly, Isaro touches upon love, proving to herself—and to us—that love is possible, until she has the terrifying thought that the man she is in love with and, in fact, has been living with, might—just possibly might—be the very man who is guilty of the annihilation of her family. No matter how unlikely this may be, the thought will never leave her, and so she cannot go on. Ian Palmer tells us, "There is a saying in Rwanda that Rwandans must swallow their tears. They do. If they did not they would surely drown."[6] Isaro drowns.

Although the novel never mentions a specific country, Isaro's native land where the horror takes place obviously refers to Rwanda. Yet a *Vogue Italia* (March 18, 2011) interview with Gatore tells us that "... even if his novel was written from the desire to reconstruct his lost diary, the author says he is bored with brutal stories: 'My book isn't a political tract—and it isn't yet another book about the poor little Rwandan.'" Indeed, it is not. It is a true artist's attempt to "comprehend the incomprehensible."[7] Like other artists, he has been if not accused of using art to do so, certainly questioned about whether and how art can possibly depict and explain genocide and, furthermore, whether this is ethically acceptable. A visitor to the virtual exhibition[8] of Kofi Setordji's memorial on the genocide in Rwanda wrote in the guest book, signing with the name Boo Fried-man, "People will never voluntarily confront genocide or crimes against humanity—It is too harsh, too incomprehensible, too cruel. Genocide can only truly be comprehended through art, of any medium." In an interview with Maarten Rens (in February 2002, in Accra), Setordji himself said, "After the genocide people lament. All they possess is what is inside them . . . You cannot break the spirit inside them and we see this spirit in the form of music and poetry." And in the fiction of Gilbert Gatore.

MARJOLIJN DE JAGER

NOTES

1. Jeffrey Brown interview with Roger Rosenblatt on *Art Beat*—PBS News-hour, January 31, 2011.

2. On-line video interview: www.dailymotion.com—ina.fr, April 14, 2011.

3. Anneleen Spiessens, "Voicing the Perpetrator's Perspective: Translation and Mediation in Jean Hatzfeld's *Une Saison de machetes*," *Translator*, 16.2 (2010), 315–336.

4. Gérard Prunier, *The Rwandan Crisis: History of a Genocide* (New York: Columbia University Press, 1995), xii.

5. Anne Cubilie, *Women Witnessing Terror: Testimony and the Cultural Politics of Human Rights* (New York: Fordham University Press, 2005), 3.

6. Ian Palmer, "Darkness in the Heart," *British Medical Journal* (August 12, 1995), 459; *Expanded Academic ASAP* (online), September 13, 2011.

7. Rhoda Woets, "Comprehend the Incomprehensible: Kofi Setordji's Travelling Memorial of the Rwanda Genocide," *African Arts*, 43.3 (Autumn 2010): 52.

8. In 2002 the Dutch foundation Africaserver.nl created an online exhibition of the genocide memorial in their Virtual Museum of Contemporary African Art.

THE PAST AHEAD

1. "Dear stranger, welcome to this narrative. I should warn you that if, before you take one step, you feel the need to perceive the indistinct line that separates fact from fiction, memory from imagination; if logic and meaning seem one and the same thing to you; and, lastly, if anticipation is the basis for your interest, you may well find this journey unbearable."

*   *   *

Your gaze falls on her, motionless yet alert. Unaware of the secret she hides you don't censure your mocking thoughts. She looks like a giant bird, the kind that balances on one foot for days on end. You dare not laugh at the image. Your presence must remain circumspect, unnoticeable.

The silky darkness, at odds with the ray of light from the window, only allows you to discern her silhouette and the profile of her face.

Her silence begs you to stay with her, and somehow you know this is not the time to refuse her anything. So you stay, frozen in place and absorbed as she is. In the settling stillness it seems that your spirits meet. Nothing you discover about her (and how would you? you avoid the question) takes you by surprise.

She remembers the first words of the narrative she had no idea would so outstrip her when she began. "Dear stranger, welcome to this narrative, whose only survivor will be you," she'd first jotted down in the corner of a sheet of paper. Then she'd hesitated. The introduction was too violent. "Don't add any verbal violence to that of the facts," she remembered. She ended up choosing words of caution that didn't satisfy her. Too indirect. Even today she isn't pleased, but she's accepted the idea of letting the text stand.

She began to write a few days earlier, the evening when, for a completely different reason, she locked herself in here. Without any warning the words spilled all over each other inside her arm, immediately demanding the repose they sought in the small note-book directly in front of her. She can still feel the trace of their violent and acrid rush through her veins. For hours before she began writing she had clutched her pencil between her fingers, like a fistful of massive tidying needs, where so many things had piled up for so long and in such disorder that she couldn't open it without everything tumbling out to crush her. Weary, she had loosened her grip at last. The sheets of paper scattered around the room are the result of this outpouring.

She isn't writing today. She has unleashed the flow of words and the thoughts they express, like bloodletting.

Useless to herself hereafter, she remembers. Like a new commander reviewing his regiment to establish his authority, she visits her memories one by one. She's afraid of indifference. She's afraid she's been defeated. But this feeling is merely a pointless reflex, for in the final analysis, it is no longer up to her to advance or retreat. She's been launched, and she'll be crushed. She is no longer anything but the example of a law of which you are the indispensable observer.

Sitting straight on her stool, an unmoving image, she thinks that if she reflects long enough and is sufficiently stubborn she might end up understanding something. Actually, she's moving among images she forces herself to register in a clear order, images upon which she hopes she will impose herself once and for all. As she thinks this she can't help but wonder whether it isn't she who is being visited, scrutinized, and subdued by her memories rather than the other way around.

ONE

2. Today, like yesterday and the day before, when night falls, Utiwonze, Uwera, and Shema come out of their holes to keep watch together. Niko, who himself is being watched by the monkeys, observes them from the opening to the cave. According to a rule that no one tries to justify, the piles of stones beneath which these three live should be seen as houses. What one really shouldn't think about are the mounds indicating the fresh graves. The whole thing should be considered a village whose name, Iwacu, exists nowhere other than inside Niko's mind.

3. Niko saw the other three people who live here in addition to the monkeys arrive one after another. Uwitonze came first, followed by Uwera. Shema was the last one to appear.

4. The cave is located at the top of the hill, which is itself an island. It lies in the center of a lake whose entire perimeter can be seen from the promontory.

5. If a stranger were to appear in the middle of Iwacu, he would surely ask himself a few pointless questions. He would wonder whether a pile of stones becomes a house by the simple fact of sheltering a human being. He wouldn't understand why these three individuals remain consistently mute and burrowed inside their shelters as long as the sun hasn't yet vanished below the horizon. He'd be astonished to find no trace of a path or a harbor on the island, as if coming and going were out of the question here. The intruder would be surprised to notice that in order to penetrate the three little mounds of earth you have to crawl feet first, like a snake

moving in reverse. The troublemaker would end up thinking that Uwitonze, Uwera, and Shema are here as runaways. He'd assume that the houses of Iwacu look like graves so as not to attract any attention. That's why there's never any fire. And that's also why the three inhabitants are attached to the silence, the disconnection, and the thinness that turn them into living abstractions. Proud of his analysis, the stranger disappears the way he'd come, without any warning.

6. "Dear bystander, if you are in as much of a hurry as this stranger you should follow him and vanish as well. This is the best time, for after these lines it won't be as easy for you as it is now to leave."

7. The cave contains the source of a much sought-after hot water spring. No one has seen it because entering is taboo. Indeed, it is said that offenders will even be punished by being permanently swallowed up by the cave's wafting breath. Water collects in a basin that has formed a little lower on the side of the hill. It cleanses everything, even gullibility. At least that's what the most trustworthy springs have always confirmed.

8. Among other pieces of evidence, the perils of the cave and the efficacy of its water are recognized both by the most respected therapists and the most ancient tales.

9. Besides the water, at the entrance of the cave where the daylight begins to make way for darkness, there is a print the length of a hefty adult male's foot. Here, too, tales provide the best information since no one is supposed to have come close enough to the cave to have seen this outline. The footprint, the story says, is that of a king who lived at a time when God still dwelled inside the entrails of monkeys. His size and strength gave him everything that his birth had forgotten to offer him. According to the legend, it was while he was visiting his land that the king passed through the island. And he put his signature on the property by striking the soil with his powerful foot inside the shelter so that the rain wouldn't erase the imprint. Ever since then, on the night that they are to become men, boys come here to ask the footprint for the strength and courage with which to mark their own life as the giant king had marked the ground. It's the only night that anyone is allowed to

disembark on the island, climb to the summit, approach the cave, and draw a little of its miraculous water. 10. That is why the island is the only place where the soil has retained its true color while blood drenched the rest of the country. Niko must have thought it a safe place to be when he came there to live. 11. Niko doesn't believe the story of the giant king. His experience and his imagination have constructed an entirely different version. The day he became a man and came to say the ritual prayer before the footprint, he didn't heed the advice he was given. He entered the cave, although he'd been told that he shouldn't, under any circumstances, either look at or approach it too closely. They had guaranteed him that he'd run the risk of being sucked up and he would disappear for good. Besides, Gaspard had added, it wasn't just a risk, but a certainty, for all the known tales were adamant on that point: none of those who'd been too curious or foolhardy had ever come back.

12. In spite of all these warnings Niko couldn't resist the urge to take a few steps inside the cave, or else curiosity and regret would have killed him. On that particular night, by the light of the torch they'd made for him to avert animals and demons, he'd moved forward into the darkness, holding his breath in terror. He'd barely begun to advance when he saw a shadow flee ahead of him. As he ran, the vision made him give free rein to the fear he'd been able to control until then. The size of the cave echoed the sound of his steps that, multiplied tenfold, made him run even faster, and he sweated as he'd never done before. Once outside, he realized he'd dropped the torch but didn't dare go back into the cave to find it. When he returned to the village he told them that he'd been forced to throw it at an animal that was threatening him.

13. Could there be a link between the fate that constitutes a life, a secret breath that might guide its trials and errors? Is it possible that in reality life has a direction that everyone simply follows? Why was it that Niko, who would find refuge in the cave later on, defied the taboo of entering it?

14. Niko didn't tell anyone about his adventure. He'd committed a desecration, and if on top of that he'd broadcast his audacity

he would have been severely punished. But his experience in the cave continued in his innermost thoughts. What was that creature that had run away from him? It wasn't any ghost or monster, for it wasn't anywhere near as big as he. Of that he was certain. Perhaps it was only a cat or a rat that had terrified him so. That hypothesis made him think again of his mad dash to the cave's entrance that now seemed painfully ridiculous. Was it to exorcise this shame that he returned to the cave?

15. Niko also remembers the reverberation his footsteps had made, which gave him the feeling of being in an infinite hollow. An echo whose muffled and interminable vibrations continued to resonate inside his head for years. Had he returned to the cave to overcome that insistent vibration?

16. The night he'd felt that shameful fear he'd left the cave too quickly to know what it looked like. Judging by the sound, he was sure it was immense, and his imagination had done the rest. At first he pictured the cave as the entrance to an unknown subterranean village of which the hill and the island were merely the roof. But soon this theory seemed too basic to him. Before long he preferred thinking that the cave was simply the beginning of a path allowing you to travel to the center of the earth, and in reality the latter was only a superimposed infinity of worlds. A secret passage. The cave would have to go very deep and come out above the clouds of another world. Similarly, when his imagination rose above the clouds, it ended up encountering a vault that was nothing other than the floor of a new world. That idea pleased Niko and in these new universes he could let his imagination run wild. This elsewhere, which in his mind was fleshed out more every day, became so interesting in the end that he spent most of his time there. Nothing is more delightful, he'd say when he came back to himself, than living inside a universe you have created.

17. There was no light in the world whose entrance Niko was so happy to have discovered. Life was expressed in the form of vibrations that governed three different states: rest, action, and meditation. The beings living there were shaped like bubbles floating from one state to the next according to a spontaneously balanced distribution. Thus, everyone was always at ease.

Niko liked thinking he was one of those bubbles. Nothing is more delicious than being an element of a world you have invented yourself, he kept saying. Was it to escape from those who found his reveries too disquieting and to live fully inside his head that Niko had chosen to find refuge inside this cave?

18. If Niko were to hear the theories that explained his presence here he'd undoubtedly be embarrassed. He might even get angry. How can you not see the real reason for my withdrawal? he'd think. Do I have to unlock my breast so that what drove me here would be on display? Don't you smell the odor that accuses me? And the sorrow that I breathe? To express all this he'd laugh in that peculiar way of his. He'd laugh without anything showing in his face, and that inner laughter would accompany a mirthless gaze.

19. Niko's face is well proportioned and even graceful. Nevertheless, when it cracks into a smile, which hasn't happened in a long time, it reveals dirty, crooked, and uneven teeth. Then a repulsive demon pierces his harmonious features. Niko knows it. That's why his smile no longer passes beyond his innermost thoughts, the enclosed compound where he lives most of the time.

20. Before he became aware of the horror it stood for in the eyes of other people, Niko used to smile a lot.

21. Is it this smile that made them call him Niko the Monkey?

22. The day he felt the urge to come and live in the cave, Niko was afraid of two things: that they would try to prevent him, or that someone had the same idea before him and was already living there. But other than killing himself he had no further solution. To assure himself he hadn't been followed or, more importantly, hadn't been preceded, he spent some time in a eucalyptus tree overlooking the slope of the hill and consequently a good part of the island. From the height of this tree he was able to observe the shrub-covered ascent through which he'd come and the slender band of sand on which he'd landed. Farther in the distance the calm waters of the lake stretched out. Farther still, the greenery began again, in whose center he tried fruitlessly to make out some place he knew. He also surveyed the entrance to the cave, especially at night when light, noise, and smoke were easier to spot. After several days, when he still hadn't noticed any sign of life ei-

ther preceding or following him, Niko decided to come down from the tree and approach the cave.

23. The first time he came here, on that unfortunate night, he'd been obliged to hold his torch at ground level to see where to put his feet. He was in complete darkness as soon as he'd crossed the threshold of the cave. He seemed like a ghost floating in black water. Everything materialized at the last moment, just to scare him. He could see no further than his outstretched hands palpating the darkness around the luminous halo inside which he was moving.

24. This time Niko waited for the daylight. It ultimately changes nothing since the light abandons him as soon as he's inside the cave, but he feels more secure. Knowing what to expect, he didn't forget to bring a torch.

25. Since the day he should avoid thinking about for fear of feeling dreadfully ashamed, he has given up on various expressions that normally animate the human face. Gradually, he's replaced them with a single expression that he now wears like a mask. Besides, to anyone not paying particular attention, Niko's head would look like a real mask.

26. What is it that could have brought Niko to keep his face frozen in such an enigmatic contraction? Is it the same reason that led him to return to the cave?

27. The mask Niko displays as a face seems to be sculpted out of hard wood covered with a brownish, fairly uniform patina. It is topped with a rug of raffia fiber, surely meant to represent a head of hair. Wide, black eyes are outlined below a smooth forehead. One could assume that in the past they must each have been bejeweled with a diamond. From the center of these eyes juts out a long nose with small nostrils. The hollows of the mask's cheeks emphasize the high cheekbones, each decorated with two prominent lines that suggest scarification. Finally, the sculpture displays a diamond-shaped mouth formed by thick lips surrounded by fine specks hinting at a beard. This mask is Niko's face today. The rest of his body is wrapped in a bulky, grayish cape, from which protrude two slim, dry legs set upon large bare feet.

28. At the moment, the most noticeable difference between a mask and Niko's face lies in the hunger, the exhaustion, and the guilt that cannot afflict a mere piece of wood with such intensity.

29. After his watch from the top of the tree, he assured himself that the cave was empty by pricking up his ears in front of the entrance and standing motionless longer than even the most seasoned hunter would have tolerated. All he heard or saw were insects, water, bats, and small animals that were probably rats or wild cats or both. But since his mind is not happy with the evidence, Niko decides to assume there must have been a monster, too, that had fled at his approach. If it's true that monsters sense invisible things, as fables describe them, it's normal that it would have frightened him. As always, Niko soon finds his first assumption too simplistic. In fact, when he starts to listen to the cave with complete attention he feels a breath. A breath that's as light as it is regular. What if the island and the hill were only the projection of the nose of a giant who drowned in the lake? The shock of his head against the bottom of the lake could have knocked him unconscious without finishing him off. And what if in reality the two volcanoes in the distance were the feet of this same giant? And couldn't the series of hills that rise from the lake here and there be the arms of the colossus? To end his description, he imagines that the head split by the shock must have dissolved in the lake, leaving only the nostril that stubbornly keeps breathing. It is this nostril that had shaped the cave in which he was going to seek refuge.

30. How is it possible to imagine that a hill and a cave forming an island in the middle of a lake are actually the remainders of a half-dissolved but still living giant? To Niko such a concept comes as naturally as thinking that two and two make four comes to others.

31. Convinced that he's alone, is Niko really satisfied? Wouldn't he like to meet the monster, of whose presence he has always been assured, so he can be devoured and finally relieved of the hunger, exhaustion, and above all the nausea that torture him?

*   *   *

The room is dark, yet welcoming: a strange mix between a place to live and a place to work. She holds herself rigidly, and one has to pay close attention to make sure that she's not a mannequin. Sitting amidst a mound of papers, notebook and pencil in hand, she's not writing. She's looking through the narrow window.

Methodically, she starts by recalling how it all began. At times she loses the thread. She no longer knows what brought her here. Often she even tells herself that she's made a mistake, a "fine fuck-up," as the other one told her one day.

The other is the one who was important at some point but would be crushed today if he were aware to what extent he no longer means anything to her. But in her inner dialogue she recognizes this is an always-fleeting doubt. She knows that being here can't have been a mistake. A mistake happens only when you have several options. She isn't sure she ever had a choice.

She remembers the morning when everything began, she is now certain of that. That morning is set firmly in a recess of her head. Every now and then she likes to take it out, the way you unfold an old garment to let it breathe, consider its wear and tear and its obsolescence. Almost indifferent, she sees it unfurl again, as precisely as possible.

It's a typical morning. A strident ringing wakes her. Seven o'clock. A few minutes later, she gets up, slowly. She puts on the kettle and lights a cigarette. She takes a shower. She gets dressed after spending a minute, dazed, in front of her closet. She has cereal and drinks tea. She gathers up the things she needs for her classes and goes off to catch the 8:10 train. A typical day also means that she puts on makeup before leaving while the small apartment whose window she has opened fills up with fresh air from outside and that she turns off the clock-radio whose sound has been her companion since seven o'clock. Usually, nothing of the flow of news, weather reports, commercials, and songs reaches her foggy consciousness. Just like her yawns, the shower water, or the tea, the radio is only a means of stimulating her sleepy senses.

As she remembers it she is alone that morning. The other one hadn't inflicted himself on her for the night. Before picking up her briefcase she makes sure she has everything she needs. She almost left the report she'd prepared for the marketing strategies course on her desk. She congratulates herself on her habit of checking everything before going out. How does an involuntary action manage to slip into an automatic physical function?

When she goes to turn off the radio before leaving, she raises the volume instead of turning it down until it clicks off. As unbelievable as it may seem, it's because she increased the volume rather than turning it off that she is now here. Everything else flowed from that gesture.

She remembers exactly how violently the sound burst forth. She wonders whether it's possible the sound never even left her ears from the day that she's now revisiting in her thoughts. Besides, where does the sound go that we hear? Where do words go once we've heard them?

That morning the radio shouted at her that, in a country of which the mere mention made her freeze with anxiety, the number of prisoners was such that, at the speed with which the verdicts were pronounced, it would take two or three centuries to examine each of the cases. More softly now that she'd turned the volume down, the reporter quoted the percentage of the incarcerated population in proportion to the population of the country itself. He was talking about her native land.

She stared at the small clock-radio for a very long time, her gaze seemingly directed at a friend who had just betrayed her in the most shameful way. Until that moment she had managed to protect herself from the mere mention of the only word that was unbearable to her—the name of the country where she was born—and she couldn't understand why she had failed. She ended up turning the radio off, but the news item on the air that had assaulted her the way a criminal pounces on his prey wouldn't leave her.

As she was walking toward the station, it seemed to her that she was having a more difficult time than usual hurrying along so she wouldn't miss her train and her first class.

In retrospect, it was apparent to her that at that moment, as she was dragging her feet going to school, she had already moved on to something else—to another place. She was merely going through the motions, fulfilling a routine, or doing something she still saw as a duty. But part of her was no longer following along.

She arrived a few minutes early anyway, even though she wasn't rushing as much as she usually did. In the lobby a crowd of students was milling about and rustling like a disturbed anthill whose population had suddenly grown and whose sound had been amplified.

Some were falling all over each other to catch a glimpse of the screen that showed which courses were being taught in what rooms;

others were waiting their turn at the vending machines selling drinks. Most were chatting and smoking.

She is pleased to note that this world, though it couldn't have changed in any way, has become completely foreign to her today. It's only in a dream that she goes back there, joins up with a cluster in the lobby, and, after the obligatory round of kisses, hears herself ask the question she had formed:

"Did you hear the newscast this morning?"

No one picked up on her comment so she began again:

"Did you hear that unbelievable item on the prisons?"

"Yeah, you mean about those massacres a few years ago? What do you expect, such horrible events implicate an awful lot of perpetrators, and so an awful lot of prisoners. It's only normal."

"What do you expect?"

"It's terrible, but what can you do . . ." a voice added in a compassionate tone, raising his hands and dropping them to his thighs, as if to bring the conversation to an end.

A short silence followed this remark that had escaped everyone except her. She plummeted down inside her head, feeling as cumbersome and painful as a brick in the pit of her stomach would be. Her brain sap was trying doggedly to rein her in, to no avail.

When she resurfaced from her straying thoughts, the conversation had picked up again. Everything she heard made her nauseated. A burden similar to that which had kept her from running for the train that morning added to the throbbing in her head, immobilized her. She was incapable of going to class with the others and even less of giving a presentation, as she was expected to do. So she headed outside without alerting anyone, her face showing nothing unless someone could see how haggard she looked.

She slipped her student ID card into the door detector and abandoned it there. As she walked toward the station, the words of that one phrase etched themselves into her head, flickering as on the screen of an old computer on standby: *It's terrible, but what can you do . . .* Had they said it to hurt her? Did they know, or were they making fun?

She felt like crying but restrained herself. She didn't care to add another drowned face recovered from the water to all the ones in front of her in the train going back. She'd bought a newspaper should she lose control. She opened it and buried herself in its pages, too much so to look as if she really were reading. Had anybody been interested, he would have seen that she was trying above all to hide what, that morning, had so dramatically illuminated the absurdity and cowardice of her daily pattern. She lost her grip and ended up by shedding at first two tears, then four, until she stopped counting them.

Once home, she threw herself on the bed and closed her eyes for as long as she could. And she had wept and wept and wept.

That morning, whose every detail she is replaying, she blamed herself first of all for not getting a hold again of the enthusiasm that had always carried her forward. Then, imperceptibly, something else got in her way. She was taking pleasure in feeling lost, crushed, trapped—commendable for once because, satisfied to drop the mask, finally naked, this excess was not acquiescence.

TWO

32. The cave Niko discovers resembles the one he's spent years imagining in almost no way at all. When you enter it, the passageway widens as you move forward, opening into the first hollow space. His immediate plan is to make that his living area. Light and wind sometimes come this far, faintly, which eases the darkness and humidity. From the entrance to the cave it is impossible to see the high recess to which he will attach his bedding. Suspension is the only way to be protected from the animals and insects with which he must share his cave, he observes, congratulating himself on having brought twine with him. Yes, hanging the bedding is a good idea: the swinging movement of the setup will be enough to keep bats, rats, and cats at a distance. Cockroaches, spiders, and ants won't be able to get at him except via the fastening point, and he promises himself to keep a particularly watchful eye on that. And if there are any mosquitoes and flies he'll just have to get used to them. In the back of this first hollow space, a passageway he is forced to crawl through opens onto the ceiling of a very large room. Before he's able to get down into it, Niko must first braid a long cord and attach it pretty firmly so that he can use it to climb up and down. So he goes out again to gather dried banana tree bark, which he dampens in order to work it without cracking the pieces, and from this he makes two long ropes. Still farther down the slope he finds a long stalk of bamboo, which he thrashes against the ground to soften it up. Three ropes are bound to provide him with what he needs to get down into the second hol-

low area. The twisted bamboo stalk assures solidity while the banana fiber cords will facilitate his grip.
33. Niko isn't comfortable in a place that he hasn't thoroughly checked out.
34. As he makes his descent, the torch, now humid and lacking air, threatens to go out with his every move. He realizes that he can't continue his exploration and tries to go back up, but his weary arms won't support him and he falls down.
35. He thinks his absence lasted only a very short period of time. One second that stretched out indefinitely, as far as the infinity of memory, as far as the dream's eternity.
36. First he felt his arms defying, then his entire body deserting him. He remembers having let go and the awareness that his head was going to hit the ground first. And a moment later, he opens eyes that are stunned by what they've just seen and troubled by not recognizing anything in the darkness that greets them.
37. He wonders if he's really awake when a monkey approaches him. He watches the animal's silhouette as it detaches itself from the darkness. A stern face and a massive hand are displayed to sprinkle him with water and shake him before disappearing into the blackness, only to reappear soon thereafter. He muses over the scene from afar, as if it doesn't concern him, because he is trying at the same time to reconstruct the dream he just had. He sees the monkey bustle about the way you see a bird go by in the sky or an ant on the ground—without paying it very much attention. He sees him without watching him, immersed as he is in what he saw when he was knocked out by the shock of his fall.
38. In the dream, Niko was walking around the island with his father. A brilliant sun was their companion, and the forest sounds echoed their good mood. They were walking amidst splendid eucalyptus trees, banana trees bowing under the weight of their heavy fruit clusters, acacias, and bushes of fern, hibiscus, and bamboo; and there were still other plants whose names he didn't know. There seemed to be no animals at all other than a few birds swirling around, so high that their cries were inaudible. Neither was there any wind rustling through the foliage, so the silence was complete. However, nothing bothered them, and at first, they didn't notice that the forest around them was being transformed as they wan-

dered through it. Slowly the trees were growing longer and lining up to form columns, centering on the spot where they were standing. At the same time, the wild grass had been brought down by the soil, and the birds flying in the distance were coming closer. They were crows. In the dream, the trees—ever taller and leafier—ended up eclipsing the sun's brightness, and soon only a dark and viscous red was breaking through the foliage. In the grip of this terror, frozen with fear, Niko and his father watched what was going on. The trees, now altered into human shapes, were forming an army of motionless, silent giants. No longer able to control his panic, Niko cried out. He wanted to tell his father that they had to run, but instead of a voice, flames came from his mouth. The flame first set fire to his father, who, before he succumbed as he choked on the smoke, asked, "Why, my son?" Very quickly the fire reached the giant figures that had once again turned into trees, and everything burned up except Niko. When the fire died out, Niko saw nothing but a charred expanse and a grimy sky as far as the eye could see. Even the lake had dried up. At that very moment a warm rain began to fall. Raising his eyes to the sky, Niko felt it shower on his face before he saw the monkey spit on him and shake him. He still didn't know whether the darkness he saw was the continuation of the opaque fog the fire had left behind or whether he was now awake.

39. It's impossible to know how long Niko lay there in the dark, at first unconscious, then mesmerized by the view of a monkey appearing and disappearing into the shadows, and finally engrossed in the recollections of his dream. Generally speaking, with Niko it's impossible to have a reliable temporal reference point because he himself doesn't think it's terribly important, among other reasons.

40. The fall and the dream remind Niko of something. A confused memory. The monkey comes back. Again. He spits on his face, shakes him, and leaves. Suddenly Niko understands it's water. The monkey keeps going to the spring to fetch it and then sprays him to wake him up. With that thought in mind Niko comes back to earth. He no longer sees the animal as an abstract presence but as a real being that from now on he will associate with specific memories. "Monkey," he mumbles. "Water . . . cave . . . rope . . . torch," he continues, and remembers very clearly where he was, why he'd come here, and how he'd fallen.

41. He doesn't have the strength to be scared of the animal. What energy he has left is consumed by the pain pummeling away at the top of his skull and the other one ripping at his stomach. This anguish awakens a memory in him that slips away as soon as it's stirred up. He must avoid certain thoughts.

42. He hears cries. The swarm comes closer and, suddenly, there are some twenty monkeys, big and small, surrounding Niko, turning him into a plaything. He doesn't have time to be frightened when a multitude of curious, noisy fingers are exploring his nostrils, ruffling up his hair, pulling at the skin of his belly, tickling his feet, twisting his penis, and stuffing soil in his ears. Niko has to get up if he doesn't want to risk winding up as a shapeless human paste. The idea has hardly taken shape inside his head when the unruly hands grab him and throw him in the air once and then even higher a second time. Forgetting the uproar, the pain, and the exhaustion for a moment, he understands he's being flung the full length of the rope. At the third try he grabs hold of it and, after some long, painful, clumsy writhing, he manages to cling to a nearby edge of the passageway that leads to the first gallery. He almost falls several times but the whooping, which he interprets as encouragement, helps him hold on. Having finally made it to the passageway that should allow him to get back to the first hollow area and then to the outside, he turns around to thank the monkeys, but they've vanished. All he sees behind him is the rope swinging above a dark and silent hole.

43. The pain, hunger, and guilt that dig their pincers into him don't leave him any time to wonder what just happened. Did he really run into monkeys down there? Was he cheered on, booed, ridiculed, or driven out? Does the cave continue beyond the expanse into which he'd fallen?

44. According to a fable whose details he can't recall, there was a time when humans and monkeys of all kinds formed a single family. That was the day mankind began to think bad luck had come to earth. The tale draws the conclusion that whoever wishes for happiness must stop talking, dreaming, and thinking, in that order. Monkeys in general are said to be the guardians of this lost wisdom—gorillas in particular, since they have always kept to themselves, away from the snare of thinking and dreaming and of words above all, content instead to see, understand, and do.

45. For a while some people nicknamed him Niko the Monkey because they thought that, being mute, Niko could neither think nor dream.

46. To provide a basis for the comparison there was his smile, too.

47. Niko crawls to the outside. When he arrives at the edge of the small basin where he can quench his thirst, he sees that the luminous full moon is perfectly reflected in the mirror the water forms. He brings his lips to it, gently, so as not to disrupt the sublime vision. When at last he decides to listen to his senses rather than to his delight and drinks, his head, his stomach, and the nausea settle down.

48. It's not so much the water per se, he makes himself think, but the bits of moon steeping in it that bring such comfort. He lies on the ground, legs and arms spread wide, chin planted firmly on the muddy edge of the basin, his eyes unseeing and his tongue extended at regular intervals to lap up the delicious water. He would be perfectly happy if time could stop and freeze him in this position, in this feeling. If he had no stomach, if the daylight wouldn't come, and if he weren't afraid to be attacked or to rot in this pose, he could undoubtedly live like this forever. To see the image of the moon floating before him, blur it from time to time as he dips his tongue, feel the coolness flow through his body, and wait for the image to find its purity again before disturbing it anew. To not be concerned with time. If happiness exists it must be something like this. The thought glistens in his head like the moon's reflection in the basin in front of him.

49. Night has fallen, and the moon in the black water has become a small, gleaming lozenge whose radiance is heightened by the stars that look like motionless bubbles. Niko ends up seeing it as a manifold blur.

50. Happiness is what you are forced to abandon. That's what he tells himself when he finally gets up.

51. How much time passed as he lay there, stretched out, with empty head and belly, distracted by the image of the water mirror? Long enough that he'd grown unaccustomed to standing upright and had to stay seated for a moment as he readjusted to keeping his head higher than the rest of his body. He tries to steady his feet. That's when he hears a familiar ruckus. On a rocky mound

the monkeys get restless when Niko appears behind a hillock not far from them. They come hurtling down the slope, and Niko staggers after them, just a few strides behind. A voice deep inside tells him to trust the monkeys. His heart seems sure that their destinies will be linked from now on. He's certain they will guide him to the closest food.

52. "He who doesn't know how to act observes, listens, and becomes kind," confirms a saying he's not thinking of.

53. On the ground, melons roll on their juicy curves, and bunches of bananas give off an enticing perfume high up. The monkeys pounce on the bananas, and, since it's what he'd rather have but also to keep his distance and stay on the ground, Niko eats the melons. He grabs one fruit after another and splits them against a large stone beside him before scraping out the seeds and the flesh with his teeth. As he eats his fill, he's in less of a hurry, choosing the heaviest and most aromatic fruit. In the end he even takes the time to slice them properly with the machete he's still wearing on his belt and to throw the seeds away. The monkeys are devouring the bananas in silence. They seem uninterested in Niko, who studies them from a distance.

54. Satisfied, Niko lies on his back amidst the melons and their remnants. The rough leaves scratch his arms and legs, but he's not paying them any mind. He's looking for the moon in the sky but finds only a vague light veiled by an unmoving cloud. Happiness, he thinks, is a man forgotten by the others, his natural needs properly sorted out, comfortably settled down to feel the regular beating of his heart, listen to the distant noises, and admire the moon and the stars.

55. What's happening that, without any transition, the images of the killings resurface and stiffen him in that convulsion that always leaves him with the look of a drowning victim who's just been rescued from the water?

56. At the same time, there's the rumble of a detonation, and with it the fruit that Niko had dropped beside him explodes. Overwhelmed by a flood of unbearable images and in the grip of tremors, he's unaware of what's happening and remains flat on the ground. Dimly some kind of commotion reaches his ears. Another blast and the dust surging forth beside him bring him back to himself and

to what's glaringly obvious: they're shooting at him. And yet, as if this assessment didn't really concern him, Niko doesn't budge, a rock among the rocks, a melon among the melons. In the center of his expressionless face, his eyes, still staring at the sky, reflect the moon's discarded glow.

57. Another explosion, and this time its discharge penetrates him while a terror tempest lifts him up. He slides behind the rock on which he'd been splitting melons just before. Hugging his bent knees, burying his head inside the ball he's formed, and holding his breath, he focuses on locating the monkeys by their sound. Could they have left without him? And what if all this were merely a trap meant to eliminate him, the intruder that he is in the cave? Is he right to trust them?

58. Noticing that he's in the same position in which he had surprised so many of his victims, he's once again overcome by a flood of memories that sicken and exasperate him to the point that he vomits out everything he's just eaten. The bits of melon that stream onto the ground are still intact.

59. The firing stops but Niko doesn't feel safe, and so he waits. Even if he must wait several days before he can be sure it's safe to stand up, he's prepared to do so. Patience has always been his primary quality. After a lengthy silence during which, in addition to being watchful, he must avoid falling into the snare of his drifting thoughts, a groan catches his attention, growing weaker and weaker and more disjointed. Like a wary turtle, he carefully exposes his head so he can hear better; then, to pinpoint where the sound is coming from, he crouches to let his sweat-covered forehead, and then his eyes, glance over the rock. A few steps away lies a monkey, a bullet in the back of its head. The flowing blood forms an opaque puddle around him. Its position leads him to infer that the animal was hit as he came running in the direction of the spot where Niko was lying. The scene, sanitized by the pallid light of the moon, doesn't seem real enough to unleash the avalanche of ominous thoughts lying in ambush deep inside Niko.

*   *   *

She roams around inside her memories as in a place that is both familiar and unknown, a house fallen into darkness where she searches for markers by feeling her way. In this half trance, she sees herself, a different self, stretched out on the bed, intoxicated with confusion and her surrender to sadness. She lies there for a long time, and it is the ringing of her telephone, she recalls, that draws her from her inertia.

A friend suggested they go to the theatre that evening. Since she couldn't remain lying on her bed indefinitely and had no idea what to do next, she accepted the invitation. The voice on the other end of the line was clearly delighted, and she had trouble responding to it. It was always the same voice that showed up when things weren't going well with the other one, the voice she also associated with the most substantial discussions: Victor's voice.

The play presented a man with an incurable disease whose unpronounceable name hinted at a connection to the country that had so harshly regained her attention that morning. She could easily identify her mother tongue even if she didn't know how to speak it. In the play, the man was visited by his guardian angel, who suggested that, while he was awaiting death, he spend his time collecting inside a small box everything he wanted to leave behind of himself, everything that he'd want to be associated with afterward. The play's title was *In Memory of Him*. For some reason she didn't admit to herself at the time, she thought it was beautiful but hard to take and disturbing. A few years later, sitting at her desk, she thinks she knows why the show had been so gripping. Perhaps that was the moment when the link was formed between the revulsion that had submerged her and the project to which she now devotes herself thousands of kilometers away.

After the play, she invited Victor to have a drink. At first she was surprised that he didn't seem to have heard the news that had so shaken her that very morning, and, powerless to think about anything else, she only half listened to his comments on the play. Still, he came to it in the end:

"Did you hear those unbelievable figures on the prisons in your country? It seems that the number of prisoners is so enormous and the legal authorities so overloaded that it will take several centuries to handle all the cases."

"Yes," she answered, feigning the same neutrality as if she'd been told the score of the cricket world cup.

"It's really incredible, all the same, that such a situation can exist. It gives you a terrifying idea of the violence in that country but also of the indifference that obscures it all. It's as if a crime were committed in France resulting in the imprisonment of the entire population of Lyon and no one would care."

"It's terrible, but what can you do . . ." she uttered, to see his reaction.

For a moment he held the glass he'd just picked up to his lips, put it back down, and yelled at her, "You're appalling!" She smiled at him, and then he understood she wasn't speaking seriously.

What he said was exactly right: what she'd just expressed, which is what she'd heard that morning from the mouth of a classmate, was appalling. That's what had shocked her in the sentence: the world's obscenity, not in the display of horror and injustice but in the attitude of those who could find nothing else to say in reaction but "It's terrible, but what can you do . . . ," who could do nothing about it except allude to it between a sip of coffee and a little joke, as they'd invariably become indignant over it before moving on to something else, to normal life. That's what she could no longer deal with, that way of being resigned to every upheaval, of not letting themselves be shattered at the risk, they thought, of adding their own misery to the already-crushing wretchedness of the world. Suddenly, the attitude she had been so lovingly taught and in which she had wallowed so comfortably for years made her sick. But could it be any other way?

Perhaps, she thought as she came back to Victor who was still dwelling on how unacceptable he found the situation, that was why she'd always had a special feeling for him. He was always moved, even if it was just limited to words, and he'd always react while drawing the attention of the indifferent to the issue. That's already something.

She can't understand why she'd managed to be insensitive to the world for so long. How many times before today, when her normal routine had fallen apart, had saying "It's terrible, but what can you do . . ." been enough for her as well? How many people have, and will always have, no other reaction but that? Would she still be among them if the volume on the radio hadn't shattered her routine?

She sighs and goes back to her memories.

The interminable discussion and her walk back brought her home at the break of dawn. But instead of sleeping she began to write. That day had just made her decide to embark on a crucial project. Writing the summary of this undertaking couldn't wait. She concentrated first on writing the title in calligraphy on a separate sheet of paper: *In Memory of* . . . It took her a solid hour before she was satisfied with the result. At the time she thought she was following her usual meticulous ways. Today she knows she was mostly taking the opportunity to reflect again, to pay attention to the detail of her idea at the same time that she was paying attention to the curves of the ten letters. Beyond the project itself, she was preoccupied with other things.

In particular, she became aware that the primary result was that she'd need to abandon her studies, which had now become inconsequential. The interest of market finance, logistics, and other management controls was dissolved in the idea whose title she was carefully composing.

The next thing was that her parents were not to know. An obvious necessity.

They'd taken her in as an orphan of the tragedy when she seemed doomed. She knew how different her lot would have been without their inexplicable generosity. She would have never known any tenderness; she would have never had the benefit of all the attentions she'd been given until this moment; she wouldn't have studied with the brilliant results for which everyone gave her credit. They had been considerate enough to let her keep her name, Isaro, and, together with her color, that was the only sign preventing her from assimilating into their family. She never took the trouble of explaining that they were her adoptive parents. Better than a family, she often told herself, they were angels. Rescuers and providential protectors whose wings had allowed the little pearl that she was that had been cast out of the water to continue to grow.

Nevertheless, at a given moment that she has trouble identifying, their relationship came undone, thread by thread, until it was no more than an abstraction, just enough to keep the illusion going of a reality that had actually disappeared. For a while, the photographs they'd look at and would take endlessly formed the one and only pillar of their vanished family. The day she decided to leave and study in Paris, neutrality collapsed. Her parents were merely disciplinarians who flung stifling pieces of advice at her, by telephone and every day. She eventually screened their calls and then changed her number. From then on their sole connection consisted of the automatic monthly deposit from their bank account to hers. Because of it she was able to keep living in the capital city and soon, she hoped, to buy her plane ticket.

Now she tells herself that having behaved towards them in that manner had been foolish. She regrets it, even without thinking she could have acted differently. She believes that the alienation and then the rupture were born from an inevitable misunderstanding: everything her parents would do to anchor her in life removed her further from the only thing essential in her eyes. The more she realized what seemed for them to be the ultimate objectives or guarantees, the more she suffered from wasting her energy on running after titles that, no matter what, were unjustified. She wrongly confused them with the malaise that they made her suffer. They never stopped loving her, even in the silence she had imposed on them, which they never violated although they could so easily have done just that, by stopping the monthly deposits, for instance.

Would she be capable of loving someone in spite of herself? Would she be able to resist the desire to treat the person for whom she'd done everything, and who in the end would prove to be as insolent as she was toward her parents, as an ingrate and punish her? Was that wholehearted, unconditional love a characteristic of guardian angels?

THREE

60. When the first two shots rang out, the monkeys had scattered into the forest, while Niko remained sprawled among the melons. Had the one monkey come to him to wake him up and flee with him? That's when the shot, which must have been intended for him, had struck it down, Niko tells himself as he decides to approach the animal, whose moaning has stopped. He recognizes him as the same one who brought him back to consciousness the day he fell into the cave. He could recognize that massive body among thousands. It startles him to see that the expression on the monkey's face hasn't changed, as if death hadn't really affected it. Were it not for the wound and the blood, you might assume he's merely sleeping, Niko thinks. Perhaps that's peculiar to those whom death catches by surprise. They don't have time to see the end coming to annihilate them and to make the same grimace as those who are aware they're dying.

61. Niko knows the face characteristic of those who're dying all too well. He has embodied the warning often enough to take note of the common denominator in the expression of a prey. But he mustn't let that sort of thinking run away with him.

62. He prefers wondering whether this monkey was his guardian angel. He thinks it depends. If you must deserve it then the answer will certainly be negative. Is the death of a guardian angel a sign? Why do you need a guardian angel?

63. When Niko gets back to the cave, dragging the monkey's body behind him like a bag of rubbish, he is exhausted. He started

out by carrying and dragging it before realizing that his strength wasn't up to the task. Then he tried to roll it along, but the monkey's heavy, rigid body wasn't very well suited to that technique. Yet one thing seemed very obvious to him: there was no question in his mind of abandoning the corpse of the monkey, the animal who'd saved his life twice and paid for it with his own. That's when he sat down to think things over.

64. Do you owe your guardian angel anything?

65. The image of the goats came to Niko like a flash of light. He remembers following his uncle Gaspard, who'd occasionally leave the village with restless, fully clad goats and then bring them back hanging across his shoulders, stripped and silent. The gleaming tip of a machete would always show above the edge of the bucket he carried in one hand as he left, and then upon his return would expose the animal's bloodstained skin. One day, because his uncle had resolved to cut the throat of an animal Niko treasured above all, he'd followed him.

66. Niko had tried to teach that goat to speak. To gain the animal's trust, he'd started by giving it a name. He picked the name Niko, like his own. Then he decided to live like him, which he saw as the only way to understand what made him tick. And so, for several months, the two Nikos, inseparable, spent the better part of their time together, feeding, grazing, and chasing each other around—although, where the last activity was concerned, it should be said that it was more Niko running after Niko than the reverse. At night, before going to bed, Niko took great pains to teach the baby goat the subtleties of human language. Being mute himself, there were obviously details he was unable to explore.

67. In fact, the apprenticeship was done in a way whose secret no one could claim to understand.

68. Thinking back on it, it seems to Niko that the celebration for which his namesake had been slaughtered had been fabricated. They'd simply wanted to deprive him of the only creature he loved. It remains a deep wound for him and hurts whenever he thinks about it, even such a long time afterward.

69. When he saw Gaspard come into the stable with the bucket and the shimmering machete blade on the bottom, he knew what was going to happen. Niko was going to leave whole and come back in two pieces, his skin in the bucket and the rest across his un-

cle's shoulders. He'd thought about preventing Gaspard from doing Niko any harm, but something had dissuaded him. He'd seen how the kid was put on a leash and dragged off, far away from the village. Behind the panic-stricken bleating he'd guessed at the foundations of an intelligible language, the fruit of all his patient efforts. Unobtrusively, he'd followed his companion to the brook where Gaspard's foolproof machete unceremoniously killed him with a single blow to the neck. He'd seen Niko try in vain to get away from Gaspard's firm grip, and then become motionless as if, once death was certain, the victim understood it was in his own interest to cooperate. Then he'd watched how his uncle had hung the now-inert Niko upside down to skin him and get rid of his entrails. He'd even noticed an intelligent and disappointed soul take flight from the vapor the pink flesh exhaled. While Gaspard began to wash the machete and clean the offal in the water of the rivulet, Niko had gone back to the stable, where he spent the night. From that day onward he'd never risked becoming attached to anyone or anything ever again.

70. Unable as he was to move the monkey, Niko instantly thought of making him lighter by disemboweling him as his uncle Gaspard had done with the goats. It was the only way to take him back to the cave, he concluded before he got to work. Since he couldn't hang the animal inverted, he just laid him head down on the slope so that the innards and the blood could spill out without soiling the rest of the body. Thanks to the recollection of his uncle's motions and the machete that never left his belt, it was a quick procedure.

71. The night and the pale moonlight helped him in not identifying everything that might have made him sick. The fear of seeing the monkey move and the terror of being the target of another round of shooting made him forget the odors. Finally, his lack of strength inspired him to make a mat of banana leaves on which it would be easier to pull the animal's body.

72. Why was this monkey the one who was hit, and in his presence, too? he wonders as he goes back up to the cave. Did he follow the group in order to return the corpse of his guardian angel to them? What would have happened if he'd been the one hit?

73. Niko is ill at ease when he appears on the hillock that juts out over the entrance to the cave. It's not merely the animal he's dragging behind him that bothers him. He's also wondering why

he's saddling himself with this chore. It's been a long time since he admitted to himself that his life makes no sense, doesn't need to make any sense. So why is he bringing the body back? What's he going to do with it? Why these ideas of guardian angel, these thoughts of gratitude instead of flight? Why, as he's been doing, interpret gestures that could just as well have the exact opposite meaning? What he lacks, he tells himself, is the courage to close his eyes for good rather than persist in an impossible purgatory.

74. He has to carry the corpse a few more steps.

75. As he crosses the threshold of the cave, Niko is welcomed with shrieking. He supposes it must be the monkeys thanking him for bringing back their fellow creature. What do monkeys do with their dead? Do they bury them? Do they leave them to rot right where they crumple?

76. What does it mean to the monkeys to see Niko like that, bringing back one of their own, lifeless and disemboweled?

77. Since he retreated to the cave only just a short while ago, Niko can no longer bear any noise and finds he has to make an insuperable effort to accept the rowdy gratefulness without protesting. On the other hand, isolation hasn't muddled his senses, which he realizes are growing much sharper than before. His ears discern the subtlest movements. His eyes pick up the most distant sounds. His nose embraces invisible shapes. His hands detect odors beyond the trace of a hint. As for his tongue, it tracks down indescribable feelings in the air he breathes. Because of this sensitivity he couldn't stand living anywhere other than in this cave anymore. People and their endless racket would drive him mad. Since when has he been experiencing things this way? Is it because or in spite of this that he's killed so many people? Do those who kill have a reason for doing so? And those who die? This is what's on Niko's mind when he arrives at the cave.

*   *   *

Why do the different moments in a given life make sense only after they've been lived? Is life a journey backwards, when all is said and done? In contrast to what is often affirmed, perhaps as reassurance, isn't what is ahead of you the past rather than the future? Can the before and the after be seen as one and the same thing?

Why is she thinking this? She'll need to find out . . .

She now thinks she understands what drove her to behave toward her parents the way she had, why she turned them into the enemies of her bliss. Her explanation is a bit convoluted but close enough to reality.

Her parents' generosity had taken away her power of being an orphan, of being orphaned without any attenuating circumstance—of being shattered by it or else reborn from it. They deprived her of the possibility of being submerged by sadness and resurfacing from it. Even before she realized she'd drowned, they took her from the water and gave her dry clothes and a cup of hot chocolate. They took her far away from the lake where fate seemed to have decided she should die. They pushed her to make progress and surrounded her so intensely that the lake vanished from the horizon before she could think about turning around. Perhaps she blamed them for having diverted her from grieving those whom luck had forgotten.

By rescuing her, they hadn't allowed her the ability to complain about what had befallen her. That's the very problem with angels: their generosity prevents the completion of the cruelty and absurdity to which human beings are condemned. Their compassionate wings protect and restrict. As they reminded her all too often, she ought not to forget that she was very lucky to be alive, despite everything. She had to embrace that silence and that oblivion as a way of expressing her gratitude, appearing to be happy so they wouldn't have any regrets, pretending that what she had, thanks to them, compensated for what she had lost.

For her eighteenth birthday, they had given her two binders filled with photographs in which the details of her life unfolded in chronological order. "Everything's here!" her father said, noticeably proud. Her arrival, the first photograph, in which she appeared skinny and scared, bundled up in a sweater that was too big for her. Discovering the room that was to be hers. Demonstrations organized in her name to collect funds and help other children not as lucky as she. Her first day of school. Her birthdays, confused with the date of her arrival since her real date of birth wasn't known. Her vacations. Her dances and piano recitals. Running track. And still many other events filled the volumes.

Everything was there except for what was missing—what had taken place before the first photograph, that is. After leafing through it all and thanking them, she went back to the first picture. She couldn't help crying. She let the gathering believe they were tears of joy, moved as she was by the flood of memories. In reality, what saddened her was that the careful and systematic chronicling of her acts and gestures since she had arrived only highlighted what was omitted, what had been there before all this.

Now, as her thoughts take her back there, she can formulate quite clearly what happened. An unfocused bitterness had seized her, which she first poured out over herself and her parents. She needed to feel and display the scar she had tried so hard to conceal. Little by little, she gave up on enjoying life, not that it disgusted her but because she no longer wanted to support what they had done for her development. Or rather, she didn't accept being no more than that brilliant daughter of whom they were so proud.

She began to destroy her accomplishments and hide her pleasures. She stopped her piano lessons and her dance classes, which had made her into an extraordinarily slender and elegant young girl. She no longer cared about her classes but somehow continued her curriculum in spite of herself, unraveling and exhausting the advance she'd made on others when her studies still excited her. Her parents saw she was changing but assured her they knew she'd turn it around when the critical moment presented itself. They assured her they understood that she needed to make concessions, needed to live. After all, she was reaching an age when she had to establish her freedom. They had to admit that up until now she'd been making the choices they had made for her. Their confidence drove her to despair. They didn't grasp what she was trying to tell them, so she adopted a more aggressive tone and carried on with allusions so indirect as to be almost unnoticeable at first. When she went out she'd forget to leave them the note they'd grown accustomed to. She no longer kissed them goodnight before going to bed. She no longer ate with them, always under the pretext of having something else on her schedule. In the end, since they continued to be so understanding of her, she left home and went to study in Paris. In case distance alone wasn't sufficient, she changed her telephone number. Despite all this, it seemed to her she wasn't being heard. Her behavior was seen as a delayed adolescent crisis.

It felt as if, until recently, her entire life had been a vain attempt at telling her parents, and everyone else, about her despondency.

When she could no longer take it out on them, she began to turn her back on the other person in her life. It wasn't hard since he laid himself wide open to the innumerable whims, reproaches, and frustrations she let loose on him. Very soon he was no more than a puppet she'd summon, manipulate, and reject as she saw fit. Too much in love with her, he let her. Too intoxicated with her power, she abused it, until she found him too weak to be deserving of her love.

Then it was her friends' turn. One after the other, Victor included, they drew away from her, realizing they were fighting a losing battle. The last time they saw each other, Victor confessed that he couldn't stand her anymore. She remembers more or less what he told her. He loved her very much, but she was forcing him to realize that it's impossible to help someone who doesn't love herself, if only a little. He was talking about her, of course. He had her take note of the fact she was giving the impression of putting her last bit of pride in her stubborn insistence to get lost and not accept any help. And that was unbearable to him and perhaps dangerous as well, because if he couldn't save her, he risked being dragged down with her.

Once again, Victor was right. If there's one person whose company she misses today, someone she truly misses, misses organically—that is to say, without whom she feels incomplete—it is he.

From the distance that is her new life, she also regrets the bad things she may have thought and done. But she's proud of having had the courage to leave so comfortable a life, to take on the role she now plays in which she's been happy for a while. Now that era seems distant and unreal to her.

During the time she spent working on her project and then waiting for the needed approval, she hardly ever went out except to buy books or sweets or to take photographs for her collection of foot imagery. When she'd finish, she would lie down on her bed and stare at the ceiling, where stains and dust created figures, new and different every time. She'd lose herself in this contemplation, telling herself that life would suit her fine if she could simply stop here, once and for all, without it implying any unpleasant result.

Now that all that murky water had been decanted, her behavior filled her with shame. How could she have held it against her parents, against the other person and her friends, that they didn't know how to fill the empty space left inside her by the loss of her own family, her friends, and her country? How could she not have known that what was eating away at her had nothing to do with them? Why had she needed to exclude them from her suffering and pain?

She remembers a message her parents had left on her answering machine. She hears it as an echo lingering in time and distance. "Isaro, your school gave us your number. We heard you're not attending classes and not answering your phone anymore. That worries us. Not about the classes, but about you. The bank informed us that your account is still active, so we assume you're alive and doing well enough to take money out of different machines. If making yourself scarce is what your happiness depends upon, we will accept that, but if you want to give us some news of yourself someday, please know that we will always be happy to hear from you." It was her father who'd spoken, slowly and distinctly as if he were reading a note, then her mother had added: "We miss you, little pearl. We love you! May God watch over you." She hadn't gotten in touch with them, other than to change banks. They hadn't called her again.

What she feels as she thinks about it again goes far beyond anything like shame.

FOUR

78. Niko has fallen asleep and when he wakes up he's stretched out a few steps from the entrance to the cave. A smell of flesh and blood surprises him, and then he remembers what's happened. Next to him, the eye of the monkey he disemboweled and brought back seems to be staring at him, asking him something.

79. Does one owe something to one's guardian angel? What does he need to be protected from?

80. Just as it had seemed obvious to him that he couldn't simply leave the monkey's body where it had been shot, Niko feels that he can't leave it lying out in the open like this either; nor can he bury it, which had been his original intention. So he starts to wash the body's insides and then tells himself that it would be better if he managed to stuff something into the belly's cavity and close it up again as if it had never been opened. To that end, he hurriedly searches for the longest, most pliable, fine but sturdy stalks and gathers all kinds of dried plants with which he plans to stuff the monkey. He needs a lot of them and has to make several trips back and forth to be able to restore the animal's slightly rounded belly that had made him so likeable. After filling him and sewing him up, Niko gets busy cleaning the monkey's coat, badly soiled from all the handling. By holding three small bamboo stalks very tightly in his fist, he discovers he can even groom the fur so that it ends up looking quite neat. To complete his mission it seems essential that he keep the monkey's body suspended. It's the most difficult part, but not impossible for someone whose patience and imagination

have always served him well. A few steps behind the entrance, the archway seems the ideal spot. A root showing just above it forms an effective fastener, and the circulating air will ventilate the corpse better than it can in the back of the cave, in any case. Seen from inside the space, the monkey's body looks as if it's floating in the luminous opening of the entrance. Exhausted, Niko doesn't have the strength to go see what impression it makes from the outside. He suspects that the corpse looks like a giant and probably frightening doll. Perhaps, he thinks, the monkey can keep watching over him. Now it's no longer the sickening air that enters and leaves his nostrils but rather the air of stillness, growing increasingly calmer. He falls asleep.

81. Behind his closed eyelids, accompanied by his father and an unknown woman, Niko is walking through the forest that covers the island. A radiant sky and the woodland sounds reflect their good mood. The place looks familiar to him. There are eucalyptus trees and pines, banana trees, hibiscus bushes, bamboo, tasty-looking melons, and many other plants. Niko, his father, and the woman pick anything that's edible and savor it in silence. After a while, Niko notices that he and his companions are being transformed. Heavy horns are sprouting from their head. Thick fur covers their body. A muzzle allows them to swallow melons whole. And soon they're on all fours, bleating their astonishment. An incredulous goat now stands where the woman had been sitting just a few moments before. Next to her a bewildered billy goat tries to see what's weighing so heavily on his head, frantically trying to get rid of it, but in vain. He cannot see himself but can well imagine, first in dismay but then amused and even proud, what he must look like. The load he feels on his head lets him envision two horns that must make him look quite stylish, especially if he is as vigorous as he feels. Once the surprise is gone they continue their walk normally, and nothing impedes the little group any further. Embankments, ditches, brooks, steep slopes, tree trunks—nothing resists the enthusiasm that leads them to the top of the hill, where they discover a cave. "It's the sacred cave, the one you shouldn't enter unless you're willing to stay there forever. Where those who merely approach it are concerned, destiny's plans differ," bleats the father,

frowning and lost in thought. At these words, a sudden lightning flash rips the sky apart, followed by a mighty roll of thunder. A split second later a black cloud covers the island, and rain starts to come down so heavily it seems to want to dissolve the entire earth. The lightning throws a furious glow on Niko, his father, and the woman, now wretchedly clustered together in horror. The rain flogs them relentlessly. And the lightning strikes, over and over again.

82. "Dear stranger, I forgot to warn you that Niko's mind is a wild labyrinth in which you agree to become lost and to keep trying to have faith. In a way, it's a fall to which you must surrender, an exploration of a private domain that you have to accept as unfit for visits. Then again, don't forget you are still free. You can turn back, stay here for a moment only or forever, continue to look for the exit or break through the walls of the maze to get out faster. Take all the time you need to decide, and, should you choose to go on, follow me."

83. Not knowing where else to find shelter, the two males and the young unfamiliar nanny goat bound over to the entrance of the cave from which a foul odor emanates. They try not to go in any farther than they have to in order to escape the rain. Would it be better to be electrocuted by lightning, suffocated by this smell, or sucked up by the cave? ponders Niko, who even in his dream can't keep his mind from spinning. At that moment two hungry eyes appear, looking happy that the storm is delivering a very nice meal right to the house. Collecting his courage and his lack of consideration, forgetting the tradition that requires it be the father who intervenes in such a case, Niko appears before the host of the rock, a hyena. He apologizes for not having offered the proper greetings upon entering and then suggests they clear out immediately in order not to disturb the hyena any more. Intending a pleasant tone, the hyena answers they are welcome to stay, and that it would certainly be too dangerous to be out in such weather. She proposes they get comfortable and spend the night with her, to which Niko nods his head in a way that means neither yes nor no. He seems to feel that he's simultaneously himself and the hyena. At the same time he is scared, he questions, threatens, bleats, and grunts. He sinks his fangs into the flesh of the three goats before him and feels the pain

himself since he's one of the victims as well. The goats resist in vain. At the height of the confusion he opens his eyes. Fear is pouring down his forehead in huge drops, and sharp pains are nipping at other areas of his body where in his dream he'd been pierced.

84. The monkey he sees floating in the middle of the entrance reassures him. Niko makes out a number of silent, motionless, almost reverential silhouettes all around him. Quietly he slides over to his pallet to get a better view of the cave. He discovers it's the monkeys forming a circle around their stuffed companion. It must have been their leader, Niko supposes, while he counts the heads in front of him. Thirty-six. He realizes that each of the silhouettes, even from the back or, at best, in profile, displays a distinct personality: tender, stubborn, wistful, greedy, serious, talkative; he even suspects authoritarianism in the gleam of the eyes of the female who stands closest to the suspended monkey and is carrying a baby on her belly that he hadn't seen. Thirty-seven.

85. Thirty-eight, himself included.

86. As they begin to realize that he's watching them, the monkeys turn around, one after the other, to face Niko. After a few moments, the object of their contemplation isn't the corpse anymore but Niko himself. Their eyes contain a question, an entreaty, even, he thinks. He decides to interpret it as their wish that homage be brought to their deceased leader. And, in that sense, he feels it's crucial that he find a name for him, and, of course, he tells himself he could call him Niko. Then he points his index finger at the monkey and with his most self-assured look implies he's happy to have been chosen to direct the mourning. He has an intoxicating feeling of power and for a moment even thinks he could well be on the way to becoming the new leader of the monkeys of the sacred cave. The animals aren't following his signal but are shrieking in chorus; some are actually laughing, notices Niko, drawing the conclusion that his decision has been approved. Her face set in a magnificent smile, the female with the baby moves toward him. She shakes him roughly and shoves him so that he falls from his bed, where she settles down with a knowing look. The group shrieks even louder. Niko doesn't understand what's going on, but he's the only one.

87. Thirty-eight, himself included.

*   *   *

She knows she's reaching the most unpleasant part of the evocation of her past. If you lean over her shoulder gently, you can hear in her temples that her heart is beating faster.

During her final days in France she immersed herself in complete solitude. In the center of the desert she created for herself, she would moan in grief but enjoyed feeling she was playing her part at last. She had a large quantity of supplies and books delivered, which filled up a corner of her room, and from then on she didn't open the door anymore except to go to her mailbox to see if the mailman, whom she could she coming from her window, had brought the answer upon which her departure depended. She'd read, eat, smoke, and sleep all day long. Sometimes her eyes pulled away from her to watch herself, and what they saw added to the seductiveness of the grief to which she clung as to a talisman. She needed it.

For weeks, as she waited for the mail, she had trouble closing her eyelids to sleep. When she did manage to fall asleep, she had nothing but nightmares; she'd wake up forlorn and totally worn out. When she woke, and throughout the day, she couldn't rid herself of the fatigue that grew with every wide-eyed, passing minute. To distract herself, she'd smoke, eat, and read.

Whatever her thoughts were at the time, she now knows that dying wasn't one of them. Her state and the act she committed were not a negation of meaning—quite the contrary. She was looking to inflict upon the world and upon herself the spectacle of the odd behavior that she had controlled and suppressed all too long. She tried to demonstrate her protest in the most obvious way possible. Secretly she hoped her disappearance would cause a scandal. Once she actually dreamed that they were breaking down her door to drag her out and that her transformation would shock everyone who knew her. In that dream, seeing that they finally understood, she was quivering with pleasure, and this brought her back to life.

Incarnating horror and having her unspeakable, embarrassing misery explode before the eyes of everyone—that was what she was thinking about, holding a large glass of water and staring at the pills she'd lined up on the small, low table. The ones that helped her get rid of stiff muscles after exercising too much, when she was still taking care of herself. The ones that had calmed her recurring ear infections. The ones that had taken away her abdominal pain. The ones she would take to relax before an exam. And still others whose purpose she could no longer remember. She swallowed them one after the other, as conscientiously as a drugged and starving lab bird, she noticed, who would die while tearing out his feathers one by one before hurling himself into the void.

She counted the pills just as she used to count sheep before falling asleep when she was a child. One hundred and thirty-eight. When she was done she smoked one of the three cigarettes she had left, put the two others in a pocket, and opened the window that looked out over the roof. She sat down on the sloping roof, already queasy. She was hoping that, having lost consciousness, she would roll down and splatter in the middle of her building's small courtyard. As she waited, she smoked her last cigarettes as slowly as she could. With each inhalation she carefully filled the bottom of her lungs, imagining that a few moments later they'd be free to keep her alive. With each exhalation she followed the flight, the suspension, and the fading of the white cloud.

She smiles. What lavishness was there in the enjoyment that her death inspired in her?

The only thing that escapes her from the era she's going through in her mind is that today she doesn't know whether she died or not. With all the precautions she'd taken to make sure she would die, she knows she couldn't have come through it alive. That said, she's forced to deduce that she's very much alive.

She doesn't wear herself out trying to undo the knot of this paradox—it's too tight for her—but merely convinces herself that, even without any sign to attest to it, death is never certain and definitive. Life establishes its final entrenchments somewhere in what is considered to be the corpse, and, with time, she starts her work again. Contrary to what she might have heard, this has no connection with reincarnation or resurrection, but rather with hope. It is that indomitable hope that makes the condemned walk ahead of the firing squad instead of struggling to flee like any other animal. As long as they're conscious they hope to be rescued.

FIVE

88. Usually, any little detail is enough to prompt Niko's mind to stray into endless digressions. And yet, here, nothing that goes on around him arouses any musing in him whatever. He doesn't try to figure out what the monkeys have against him nor whether he's right in interpreting their behavior towards him as revenge or punishment.

His sole preoccupation is to make himself as unobtrusive as possible, to vanish from the glance of the monkeys, especially from the harsh female. From the way she'd shaken him he felt so weakened that it scared him more than anything ever had before. Of course, the discretion wasn't commanded or indicated to him in any clear way. He senses it. At the risk of receiving a more severe punishment than eviction from his bed, he is to submit completely. He applies himself to this by eliminating every useless thought from his mind and generally abstaining from any kind of initiative. For a very brief moment, when his imagination eludes his vigilance, he sees himself as the last leg of a caterpillar, restricted to following the movement of all the preceding ones, indifferent to thought, anxiety, and feelings, since, when all is said and done, he's obliged to follow the others.

89. If Niko is the first to wake up he remains motionless until a large part of the group begins to bustle about, allowing him to stretch without attracting any attention. Similarly, his snores are never the first ones to resonate in the cave. If he's hungry he doesn't

let it show, since he isn't allowed to eat. In any case, that's what he infers from the fact that he's been hit each time he almost swallowed or tried to swallow something. It's the female with the baby who leads the group in search of food at night. Niko can follow the procession, being careful not to come too close or move too far away. He watches the monkeys eat and is only allowed to suck on a stone to produce some saliva inside his mouth and quench his thirst that way. In the end, when he does have a thought, he tries hard to suppress it as quickly and as deeply as possible so that he can remain wholly present and totally submissive. With that in mind, Niko has come to develop an almost foolproof technique. The instant a thought begins to cross his mind, he moves his gaze to the monkey's corpse suspended not far off and that, now withered and disjointed, merely resembles an old puppet on a scrapheap. The image fills him with profound resignation. And he becomes empty once again, watching the cave and the monkeys with an odd gaze.

90. Patiently he waits for the sign he is to follow, and, by waiting, he has the sense of slipping into a new state.

91. As it becomes his only preoccupation, waiting creates a new temporal dimension.

92. When it becomes boredom Niko plays. It seems to him that it's what the monkeys do as well. After a period of meditation, digestion, or rest, they fight, chase each other as they utter sharp cries, or else they clean their coats. Anxious above all to be as invisible as possible, Niko only plays with himself. That's when he discovers oddities on his body he hadn't known about before. For example, he notices that the flesh between his skin and his bones has shrunken considerably. Wherever he touches himself anywhere other than his neck, belly, buttocks, and genitals, he immediately touches a bone. Similarly, when he presses a finger anywhere on his body, it leaves a mark behind as if it were made of wax or clay. He doesn't try to figure out what any of this means. It's just a way of forgetting time while he waits . . .

93. If a ghost were to emerge in this cave he'd be surprised first of all to see a man amidst a group of monkeys. To him, the man, visibly intimidated and malnourished, would look like a hostage—unless, he might think for a moment, it's a matter of one of those wild men whose existence some stories insist upon. The invisible

visitor would also be struck by the odor engulfing the whole cave, which must originate with the crude and so very plainly displayed mummy of a monkey. Finally, he'd notice a female perched on an astonishingly well-attached and very fastidiously wrought hammock in a corner of the space. The scene would inspire a feeling of insecurity in the highly sober intruder. Then, with the advantage of being able to do so without bothering anyone or even being detected, the spirit would get away as far as it could go.

94. "Dear partner, here we are in the middle of an uncomfortable patch. Niko is forced to give himself up to absolute passivity. He lets us conclude for ourselves that asking for nothing to be happy, that being alone, is no guarantee for serenity. Is Niko's inertia a renunciation of the hope to be at peace, and his unobtrusiveness an attempt to be erased not only from the eyes of the monkeys but from the world as well? Does he submit because he's convinced he deserves this fate? Is his self-effacement a way of dying? Is death the completion of self-effacement? In any case, one thing is certain: our presence is of no use to him at all. It may even be adding to his torment. So let us leave him to ponder the continuation, and, as we wait, let's try to get to know him better."

*   *   *

When she discovered a large envelope with the blue logo of the Foundation among the advertisement flyers, she had no doubts. It was the reply, and she didn't wait to get back up to her apartment to open it.

"Mademoiselle," the letter began, whose folds the invisible hands of her memory smoothed out to read it better. "Your project has aroused unprecedented dissension among the members of the grants committee. This is the reason why we are responding to you beyond the announced deadline. We beg you to accept our apologies for this." She remembers that as she was reading this she was surprised by the care the words demonstrated. Her file must have been quite rigorously evaluated for it to be the object of a discussion as fierce as the letter suggested. She had expected a form letter that would have informed her she did not fit the Foundation's criteria, despite the interest her idea represented. "The idea of composing a memoir about one of the events that have most marked the twentieth century is obviously praiseworthy. Nevertheless, we weren't immediately convinced: 1) that this proposal, however worthy, might not have consequences that run counter to its intention, and 2) that you have the skills to bring it to a successful conclusion. Where the first point is concerned, some of us thought that preserving even a trace of such a past would amount to preventing people from moving on and keep visible the scar and thus, too, the memories it would arouse in each of them. Regarding the second point, we thought it necessary to meet you in person first to get a sense of your abilities." At that moment she still didn't know what they were planning to tell her, whether her proposal was being rejected or accepted. "Your project elicited many other reservations as well, but none of them was sufficient for us to turn down your application." At these words she could breathe again.

Before she could go on, she had to endure the concierge's stare, openly disapproving of her appearance. She hadn't been seen for a long time and the way she looked must have been shocking. Her hair looked like a stack of metal wire piled on top of her head. Her puffy face was unrecognizable, completely disconnected from what had once inspired the concierge to pay her a new compliment whenever they ran into each other: "What a beauty!" she exclaimed one day. "How did God manage to endow one single person with so much loveliness?" That day the woman's gaze expressed a mixture of fear and curiosity, like a child in bed at night staring at a shape and trying to figure out whether it's a piece of clothing on a hanger or maybe a ghost instead. When the concierge's eyes finally disappeared behind the door, Isaro continued reading. She found out that the Foundation had awarded her the grand prize but that accepting the prize depended on a few conditions, something unprecedented in its history. "The grant will be awarded to you only if you consent to speaking not thanks to the Foundation, but together with it and in its name. In short, the idea is that you will change from being a recipient of funds to a partner." The passage disoriented her so much that for a moment she took it as a joke. The letter ended with some practical information instructing her to make an appointment with the Foundation's director as soon as possible.

She called the minute she was back in her apartment and set up a meeting for the following day.

What happened next on the day she's now remembering is much like a resurrection. For the first time since she'd withdrawn from the world, she thought about how she ought to present herself. None of her former clothes fit her any more. She tried on a few but then decided to go out and buy some things. To see her once so well-trained body defy her this bluntly made her want to laugh, which she didn't prevent. Far from deserting her, as she might have expected, her body had actually become allied with her, physically translating the change that had taken place within her. Strangely, she felt better like this than inside the small body in which she'd allowed herself to be compressed for all too long. Once she'd been to the hairdresser and was dressed, she was intrigued by the person she discovered in the mirror. As she approached the figure before her, she wondered if it was really she. For the first time in her life she thought she was beautiful.

Among the new experiences that followed the long-awaited letter, she remembers she had no need to retreat anymore. She made no effort at all to meet up with people, but neither did she refuse to go out, taking long walks in the city at night.

Is it possible that her life and her soul had linked up with a different person? Is it possible that she survived the drugs and the fall? Who was this enthusiastic young woman who presented herself to the Foundation's director and to the members of the committee that governed the grants the next day?

She was expecting a warm, considerate reception from the tone of the letter. But, although no one showed any hostility, the seven men she had to face were so excessively dispassionate that it flustered her.

With her new eyes, she recalls the scene as serious and ridiculous. The one who'd invited her in without even introducing himself and then sat down in the center of the jury had requested her to repeat her idea. This had made her shudder. Hadn't they read her file? Didn't they know about the letter? Weren't they up to date on anything? Instead of asking them these questions, she greeted them and thanked them for their attention: "I am deeply honored to be here before you to present a project that is very close to my heart. Whatever the outcome of our discussion may be, I'm already grateful for your esteemed consideration of my idea" is what she basically must have said. The man all the way to her right looked as if he knew that, with all her standing on ceremony, she was playing for time and organizing her thoughts. He leaned his elbows on the table and noisily sighed. She then came to the point with words that went something like this: "*In Memory of . . .* is a project that, to a large extent, keeps getting away from me," she announced. "Obviously, one may think that my origins, my history, my training, and whatever else preordained me to take this on. That doesn't seem self-evident to me, however. By this I mean that I'm not embarking upon it with unwavering self-confidence and that I understand the hesitation you may have felt at the time you awarded me this grant or not—a hesitation you may still feel at the present time." She rejoiced, for words had always been her favorite playthings. She paused to see if anyone approved or disagreed. Seeing no sign of either, she continued. "However, for me this doubt doesn't affect the vision I have of the project as being not only appropriate but also necessary and urgent." She very distinctly uttered each of the three adjectives, which she had jotted down on a bit of paper in anticipation of the moment they would ask her about the importance of her plan. "Appropriate because time allows the massacres that bloodied the country and plunged it into mourning to be seen as part of the past." On this point she knew she was lying, since the events certainly belonged to the past from a chronological viewpoint, but they were still present—past, but not surpassed. As young as she was, even she was still marked by them. Instead of growing blurry, of being erased with the years, and even though she'd been raised in a milieu that hardly brought them to mind, the memory of those events had been implanted and had simply grown. She'd tried to display the opposite, show detachment, rebirth, resilience, as some people told her, but deep inside her the wound had never stopped bleeding and becoming infected until the moment when she could no longer ignore it. The radio episode had merely revealed it to her.

She told herself this without losing the thread of her argument. "Furthermore, the project seems necessary since justice, for reasons that aren't mine to judge, is not playing its proper role. This results in intensifying incomprehension and resentment based upon which the seeds of a new conflict are in danger of bursting forth. The prisons are the embodiment of this powerlessness and threat.

That is why intervention in that area is a must. It is my intention to record the testimonies of every person who has experienced the tragedy: survivors, executioners, accomplices, and resistance fighters. I intend for everyone to be heard. Indeed, it's a matter of a kind of memory inventory. It will culminate in the publication of a monumental book containing every last account. The text will be saved in a computer file, and this will, of course, be reproduced and disseminated as often as needed to ensure its preservation, no matter what happens."

She must have talked too excitedly because four of the seven men were leaning backwards in their chair and grimacing, seeming to indicate she was overdoing it. In her mind she sees the man in the middle again, motioning to her with his hand and saying: "*Itonde ntacyo twari twakwangira.*" His intonation and accent were correct and stirred up images in her she thought had vanished. She was surprised he knew her mother tongue and, in order not to show it, she took a sip from the glass of water in front of her.

She continued:

"I have contacted the embassy, which has spoken to the government on my behalf. They say they're ready to consider the possibility of linking the project to the next census. I don't know whether it would be a good thing to be officially connected in this way, whether it might not denigrate the independence of the initiative for the population. Be that as it may, it is crucial to have the government's support.

"Finally, I believe the project is urgent because memories fade away, because those who have lived through that period and are capable of putting it in an enlightening historical perspective are beginning to grow older, and because the prison population with whom I want to start is in the process of being decimated by disease. Incidentally, let me make clear that what makes me want to meet with the prisoners before anyone else is my belief that, in order to understand what happened, one must hear from those who caused it. I imagine that the prisoners—in any case, those who are imprisoned for a reason—are the carriers of this cause." She was speaking fast and loud but no longer trying to curtail herself.

"Although I'm totally prepared to spend my life doing this, if necessary, I am also aware that this project cannot be completed without help. Not counting the personnel needed to coordinate it, I estimate that about fifty interviewers and an equal number of transcribers will be required over a period of five years. At the end of these five years the interviewers would be the proofreaders of the final text for another year and a half. Finally, to produce the book, the work will be entrusted to a printer yet to be chosen. The details of the projected budget are in the file."

As she said this, she blamed him, and almost showed it, for having asked her for an argument when she'd gone to so much trouble to write what he presumably had read. In conclusion, she insisted on the fact that the project "In memory of . . ." didn't claim to straighten out the country's problems. It was simply a question of giving the people a place to put down the burden they were carrying, of allowing the country to share this account, and, who knows, maybe the hatred that each individual's experience had produced might melt away. "Perhaps it is my dream that, thus acknowledged, each person's suffering will be appeased and transformed into a new cohesion," she ended.

Then it was time for questions. Although quite predictable, the first one took her by surprise: "What will be the dimensions of the completed book and how many pages will it have?" Proud of its ironic tone, the voice added the possibility of a paperback edition. She answered that she only had a vague idea about its appearance and that it would have to be discussed with the printer. The size and the number of pages would depend on the format to be chosen. All she knew at this point was that each person's account would have to consist of roughly fifteen hundred characters. She took the opportunity to remind them that it was not a matter of writing a biography of each person but to have them talk about what seemed most important to them, and whether that be a memory, a confession, a statement, a poem, a prayer, it would be a valuable view of the story. The book would essentially be a compilation of everything people wanted to say about their experience of the massacres. As far as the paperback edition was concerned, she decided not to react.

Another member of the jury asked her how she expected to guarantee the objectivity and goodwill of the testimonies. She reminded them that, as mentioned in the introduction of her application, she had no intention of turning it into a sociological or journalistic work. "Even people's lies, their omissions and exaggerations seem of interest to me. Don't forget that the objective of this undertaking is precisely that of shedding light on subjectivity, for it is on this that hatred and violence are based. I don't think that we should seek to draw the horror of these events toward us but, rather, that we should move toward it. It's a matter of showing what the attitude is of those who've lived it, how they face up to it and within it, not of telling them what their attitude ought to be."

The man who'd been taking notes since the beginning of the interview now spoke up, asking why she was so eager for the result of this commemorative census, as she'd said, to be the object of a single and functional book. Had she evaluated the almost insurmountable technical difficulties that producing such a text would represent? She replied that it was vital for the memoir to be thus composed in order that everyone could be aware his or her story had been taken seriously but, at the same time, could see to what extent it all remained relative, no matter how tragic. She wasn't sure she believed this idea. Each individual's sorrow isn't lessened by knowing it's just one among many. "Nothing will indicate who said what. The accounts will be anonymous. But people will recognize their own story and perhaps discover things in the words of others that will allow them to leave their own prison of grief, resentment, and hatred." Having said that, she added that her principal competence did not lie in the area of printing and she would leave its assessment to an expert.

To bring the meeting to a close, the director asked her when she would be ready to leave. "I am more than ready. I can go right away," she answered, trying to keep from screaming with joy. The grant was hers, is what she thought she'd heard.

They debated a little longer. They'd need to find other partners for the funding. The Foundation would take responsibility for that and would make sure that the work would be serviceable. They also needed to examine the technical feasibility of such a book and the existence or the construction of the place where it would be exhibited.

Her plane took off from Paris a few days later.

SIX

95. Ever since he was born, Niko had lived inside himself. He'd been told it wasn't a problem, and he'd never had any reason not to believe that. From the very beginning he'd been inclined to accept everything.

96. The day he was born had coincided with the rainy season, which at this latitude can be unspeakably violent. A storm had announced his arrival to a preoccupied world. While the entire household was running around in every direction to reinforce the roofing and windows, bring in the cattle, gather the children, cover the water well, and protect the fire, his mother delivered him, alone in a corner, her voice muffled by the wind blowing through the cracks and the pelting raindrops on the sheet metal roof. His mother did not rise from the hard clay floor where she offered her last gift, and for a while the newborn rolled around on the ground unnoticed. In fact, more than once he was almost crushed. His faint cries and paltry little contortions, covered up by the noise and darkness in the house, brought him no aid.

In the end, attracted by the maternal fluid, it was the dog that announced the arrival of a new being. A stunned circle formed around this tiny thing that was putting all its energy into producing an inaudible scream, flailing its extremities, while forming an awful scowl. A sense of propriety for the way in which she was laid out kept everyone's eyes away from the mother's knees. It took a moment before anyone realized she had breathed her last. Finally someone called a midwife to surgically separate the minuscule wrinkled little thing that lay squirming on the ground from its mother. In the end they rejoiced since, after all, a new member of the family had just been born.

97. At first everyone thought that the newborn's voice was obscured by the noises of the storm and the people around. Then they thought that, angry about being ignored for too long, the baby was taking revenge on the negligence of its own family members by refusing to address them in any form, not even with tears. Then some of them suggested the little one must have been shocked by his mother's death in childbirth and was expressing a certainly astounding form of mourning in the only way he could offer any idea of his suffering: through silence. Sometimes his grandmother, who never believed what she was told, would take the infant aside and ask him to please stop horsing around; he'd done a good job making them laugh but now it was enough. He had to talk or at least emit a sound; it was becoming too upsetting. She felt as if she were holding a ghastly doll that was human in every respect except for the voice, she'd admit to him when she'd exhausted her arguments.

98. Niko never showed the slightest inclination to make use of his mouth, an abandoned cavern from which no sound ever emerged.

99. When he started to walk, his uncle, a well-respected man in the village, decided to personally take on the case. He found a trick that was to put an end to the child's game: when the little boy stood up and tried to take a step, he slyly grasped his foot so he'd fall. Gaspard assured everyone that the toddler wouldn't be able to resist crying when reacting to his fear and pain. The little boy's forehead was decorated with numerous bumps but he remained desperately mute. And it didn't change when healers and doctors of all kinds came to visit, or when he was forced to take a staggering quantity of remedies, each even more ingenious than the last So they took him seriously at last and admitted it was a rare form of complete mutism that doesn't even let you cry, weep, or moan. Niko remembered all of this, for he'd retained a very precise memory of everything he'd ever known from the moment he left his poor mother's belly.

100. Since he couldn't answer, no one ever called to him, and so Niko remained nameless for a long time. To catch his attention everyone yelled at him, "Niko!" which means no more than "hey

you!" or "yo!" Because the word was associated with him, it grew
to be his name. His father, whose task it was to find a name for his
son, had no objections.

101. Niko grew up in the shadow of a woman who never called
him "son" but simply "Niko" like everyone else. She took him in her
arms only when there was nothing else she could do. Now, since
Niko began to eat like a grown-up rather quickly and the stepmother soon had children of her own, nothing further was needed
between them. So, although he could barely walk, he was shoved
out of the kitchen by his stepmother, who always had something
more important to do than give him a second of her time, and he
waddled over to his father. With a careful though firm gesture, the
latter would push aside the child that prevented him from living
like a distinguished man. To him, the idea of being a father stood
for nothing more than the duty of siring children. Niko's lot concerned him only abstractly, which is what he told himself when
he saw Niko coming out of the kitchen and groping his way over
to him. He'd wait patiently until the little one came within reach,
and then gently pushed him aside before taking another sip of the
banana wine he loved more than anything else. Still, it forced the
child into a sudden spin, and he would fall. It wasn't terribly serious
since there wasn't any risk that he'd cry and alert the whole hill-
side, as other kids did. Niko simply made do with a sad look, saw
two tears come out to blur his vision, and then got up again. Sometimes, feeling his way along, he'd go back to his stepmother who
always had some reason to find his visit unwelcome. When eventually he lost the courage to hope that he wouldn't bother them,
Niko learned to live on his own, often outside.

102. Since he wasn't good at anything else, Niko went to school
very early. He wasn't registered there since his father found it unacceptable that he should have to pay to hear some moron talk for
days on end.

The village teacher didn't protest when he saw Niko in the back
of the classroom one day. He was undoubtedly waiting for the intruder to do something foolish and then he'd throw him out. But
once inside and seated, Niko was as good as a withered plant, and
in the end, far from wanting to expel him, the teacher held him
up as the model of good behavior the others should follow. Learn-

ing that he was mute didn't change a thing. On the contrary, the teacher grew extremely fond of this student who, next to the others, seemed like a miniature but proved so much more willing to learn.

103. The teacher would have been disappointed had he known what went on inside his favorite pupil's head during class. Obviously, Niko was listening. That's why he came. But after the first day the teacher's words seemed too predictable for him to give them his full attention. Most of the time, behind an intently focused look, Niko was exploring unsuspected universes. Often his daydreams began with the same vision: alone on a deserted road, an old woman appeared to him. She'd notice him, get up, come toward him, and call him "my son." As she came in his direction, both her features and her words would change. Without Niko ever being able to grasp the stages of the metamorphosis, a dazzlingly beautiful young girl approached him and would say, "I love you; follow me." In his dream, Niko heard these words, but he wasn't moved by them and rejected the invitation. And the girl would weep tears of blood. After remaining motionless for a moment, Niko would follow her at a distance, guided by the traces her tears left on the ground as her path led him to different places, and there he'd stay as long as nothing called him back to reality. The teacher's exclamations, his classmates' whispers, and the sound of the bell at the end of the lesson always ended these journeys too soon.

104. When he came back from his mind's trip, the usual expression returned to Niko's face without letting anyone in on his distraction. In the end, it was an art at which he became extremely skillful, and he was terribly amused by the fact that the others had no clue as to what was going on inside him while the teacher was explaining some mathematical theorem or a rule of French grammar. At the same time, it made him sad that the interesting life he led existed only in his head. One day it made him wonder whether that was so because his overabundant imagination didn't allow him to find even the slightest flavor in real life.

Whatever relevance the question embraced, Niko considered himself a loner, a sort of perpetual passerby, alone and ignored. Part of his body, in the region of his belly, suffered from this incessantly.

105. At an age when his classmates were still having trouble learning to read syllables, Niko was discovering books. His teacher lent him a few, and when he'd made the rounds of his own small library, he registered him with the *bimo*, the mobile library that came through almost every month and where Niko was introduced to Tintin, Martine, Spirou, and Kouakou. After these introductory readings, recommended to him by the *bimoteur*, he quickly discovered *The Stranger, Ambiguous Adventure,* and the Bible, of which he knew the books of Genesis, Job, Exodus, and the gospel according to Matthew almost by heart; he had to read *A Thousand and One Nights* several times before he understood any of it. In addition, it could take a long time to read a book because borrowing more than one at a time wasn't possible. He didn't try to understand why he liked reading so much, even though he grasped so little of it, at least in the beginning. Reading was the only thing that fully captured his interest, the only activity in which he felt at peace.

106. One thing that's certain about Niko is that he grew close to no one during all his years in school. Of course, he might become involved in a game, or they'd call on him as a witness in a discussion, a role he fulfilled by pointing his finger and nodding his head. But these were merely interludes after which they'd thank him and he'd pursue his solitary journey again.

107. The only person Niko felt comfortable with was his uncle Gaspard. After school Niko usually went to see him work. He'd sit in a corner of the workshop and watch Gaspard, who seemed like a giant to him, facing the blazing heat of the furnace and putting in or pulling out pieces of metal that he'd strike with terrifying force with the aid of a hammer of equally large scale. Uncle Gaspard wore only what was absolutely necessary not to be entirely naked and, even so, he was in a constant state of sweat. In wonderment Niko watched him bustling about. From time to time Gaspard would glance at his nephew with a look signifying that he was thirsty. Then Niko would run to get him a gourd of banana juice, wait for Gaspard to gulp it down, take the container, and return to his observation post.

108. Niko wouldn't get up until Gaspard threw down his fiery red tongs, took off the fabric he'd wound around his hands, and held his thighs as he let out a deep dark sigh. He'd close the

small furnace door, breathe deeply for a moment, and then clear his throat from dark blobs of spit. When he'd regained a normal temperature and breathed clear air, he'd give the order for the cleanup. Niko happily obliged. In a few moments the furnace was extinguished and empty, the daily tools placed on the tray, the workshop cleaned and aired out. The last thing was to fill a small basin with water meant to dampen the protective fabric for the next day. Increasingly, Gaspard let Niko do all of this, and then he'd invite him to have dinner and sleep at his house if he wanted to. In another place, and if Niko's father hadn't still been alive, one might have called it an adoption.

109. On days that he couldn't go to school or to his uncle's or to the *bimo*, Niko was more anxious when he got up.

110. On such days he'd invent games and become so absorbed in them that it seemed they'd never end. One of his favorite games consisted of locating the boundary of a sound. For this purpose he had to find a long, uninterrupted sound, the sound of the river, for instance. He'd go right to the bank of the roaring stream and then move away until he reached the exact spot where he felt that if he took another step he would no longer hear the water's gurgle. That would really make him happy and keep that spot in mind as the outermost edge of the roar of the river's water.

Sometimes, to make the game more complex, he'd stand sideways once he'd reached the subtle borderline so that the ear on the side where the river's sound originated could still somewhat hear it, while the other ear, already beyond the limit, no longer heard anything. He then figured he'd quite accurately spotted the place where the noise he'd chosen would stop and that, in fact, it corresponded to his head. In search of the sound's boundary Niko would run several kilometers if need be.

111. The idea of teaching a goat to talk had come to him by accident, like the other ideas for games he came up with. On his way to the pottery workshop one day he'd seen a kid goat in the courtyard. Uncle Gaspard had plenty of them to slaughter and to give away. This one must have escaped from the pen. The animal had looked at Niko and then come over to him as if to say hello. With the same spontaneity Niko had approached the little animal, which didn't run away—an extraordinary thing for anyone who knows

anything about goats—and he'd picked it up in his arms. When Gaspard saw Niko come into the workshop holding the kid, he didn't hesitate. He looked at them with his soot-blackened eyes, irritated from the sweat, and said, "It's yours." Uncle Gaspard was a man of few words. To thank him Niko went to get him fresh banana juice.

112. Subsequently, Niko spent the greater part of his time with his new companion, and, to better understand him, he acted just like him from that moment on, to the point of grazing the grass in the surrounding area, suckling the nanny goat that Niko decided to see as his mother, too, and sleeping right on the ground in the pen next to the other goats. When Niko looked into the kid's eyes it seemed to him that the animal could have told him many things. That's why he began teaching him to talk. As a first bridge between them, Niko decided to give the kid his own name. Then, every evening, he focused on communicating the miracles of human language to his hoofed companion. Since Niko himself couldn't speak, the apprenticeship took all sorts of circuitous routes whose secret no one was able to discover. In any event, judging by the teacher's blossoming, the pupil's progress was clear.

A while later the friendship between the two Nikos was brutally terminated. Concerned about what the results of a relationship such as this might be, the village decided to put an end to Niko's life with Gaspard's hand. The blow that slashed Niko's neck paralyzed Niko as if he'd been in his place. For a long time afterward he continued to feel a remnant of his presence at the killing: surprisingly, the memory of the scene consolidated his body into such shaking that it could lead to blacking out. As a precaution, Niko no longer connected with anything or anyone, being content to be where he ought to be when he ought to be there.

113. After this experience, solitude, daydreaming, and anxiety found their normal way back to his life.

*   *   *

Imagine her beauty in any way you like. If it helps you to be with her, see yourself sitting behind or beside her, sharing her view over the outside and over herself. If you prefer, you're inside her, you are her eyes, her breath, or her memory.

She's looking through the narrow window, immersed in her secret wandering. She's not listening to the voices calling her from behind the door of the office she's locked herself in with you. She hears the knocks and the door handle being turned, but she ignores them.

The state she was in during the plane ride that brought her here had no connection whatsoever with anything words are likely to express.

In the course of her last few days, the other one had tried again. He'd sent her letters she hadn't even read and left messages she deleted immediately. As if he knew, he even dared to ring her doorbell the day before her departure. She'd guessed it was he when she heard the knocking without the intercom having rung first. She hadn't had the opportunity to retrieve his copy of her key.

Through the closed peephole she watched him straighten himself in the hope she'd open up. She saw him hesitate about ringing her bell a second time. Each time he'd take a step forward, move a huge, ridiculous looking finger toward the button—the effect of the wide-angle glass—then, polite and now in miniature, take a step back to wait. She saw him grow impatient, stamp his feet, and decide to ring a third time, a very long ring. Behind the door, just a few steps away from him, she was holding her breath, delighted and amused to see him so tiny when he stepped back again. When, weary now, he turned around she murmured "pathetic" in such a way that he wouldn't be able to identify where the voice came from. He'd turned back again and approached the door to ring one more time and call her name. She hadn't budged. Suddenly uncertain about what he'd heard, he listened at the other doors on the landing before going back downstairs. When she knew he was far enough away she burst out in such loud laughter that he couldn't not have heard and recognized it. Then, through the window, she saw him put the bouquet of flowers he'd brought her on a trashcan and beat a hasty retreat. She was surprised to notice that her body was tense with pleasure. She'd just felt something that she'd only barely approximated until then.

She's not sorry for having been so hurtful, but she also knows she'll never do it again. She no longer feels the need. On him she had vented the contempt she should actually have directed at herself, at the one she no longer was but which he still represented, at the girl who at one time put up with everything and anything as long as they brought her flowers.

On the plane that brought her here, she'd mostly been thinking about the flight that had taken her to France many years earlier. Her parents were returning to France, which they had left in order to teach French abroad. Completely preoccupied with what they took to be her happiness, they told her nothing else. Nor did she ask them any questions about what had happened so that only their arms were available to carry her. She didn't ask them how she'd come to be so much alone that they'd felt obliged to take her with them to save her. She didn't question them because she was afraid both that they would tell her the truth and that they would hide it from her.

After the first few years when, according to the photographs, she was the mascot at every humanitarian demonstration in the region, her arrival had been no more than alluded to. On the anniversary of her arrival date she always received a bouquet of the begonias that grew only on and around the hill where she was born. She didn't ask how her parents managed to get hold of these flowers, which were always fresh on arrival. She simply and wordlessly appreciated the sign, the secret it breathed, and the delicate gratitude it celebrated. The ritual continued until she stopped seeing her parents. Today she misses it.

The driver who took her from the airport to her hotel, unaware of her extreme fatigue after a long flight and the possibility she might not feel like talking, plied her with questions. His attitude irritated her, and, were it not for her exhaustion and shyness, she would have asked him to keep quiet and stick to what she'd hailed him to do. If she'd known what would ensue . . . Visibly blinded by curiosity, he didn't seem to notice how he was bombarding her. Where was she coming from? Did she know Zidane? What was she doing here? Where did she buy the lovely clothes she was wearing? Why was she so beautiful? Did she want him to put her up so she wouldn't have to spend money on such an expensive hotel? Had she been here before? And so on. It was almost one o'clock in the morning, and he wanted to know everything. Unfortunately for him, worn out as she was, she only responded with a yes or no.

When she could neither nod in agreement nor refute she granted him a sigh.

Luckily, it was less the answers she couldn't provide than his own words that mattered to the young man. To spare her, he suggested he'd tell her a story. She agreed, and he added laughingly that if she, the beauty, were to fall asleep he'd take her home with him. So she stayed awake. The night was pierced only by the beams of headlights and a few distant shimmers. She looked out and could see almost nothing, her posture much like the one she's in now. He took some time before beginning the story, but she wasn't paying the slightest attention to it, too engrossed in the realization that she couldn't remember ever having seen such total darkness.

Before he began his tale he introduced himself. His name was Kizito. She could see him in the rearview mirror, which he must have moved two or three times so he could better see her.

She now realizes that as early as that moment he wasn't merely a driver in her eyes anymore.

"The scene opens with an elegant swallow," he thundered, as if addressing an audience of a thousand people. And smiling, he added, "elegant like you.

"She's circling above a pond, more concerned with displaying her skills in the air and her singing talents than with quenching her thirst." He wasn't watching the road very carefully, but it didn't matter much since they were practically the only ones on it. "Finally, she sits down on a bumpy mass she thinks is a rock until it winks at her. It's a big, fat, ugly toad lazing around in the tepid water of the pond." He emphasized the description of the toad. "The frightened swallow leaps up and lays into the big, fat, ugly toad. 'What did God want to punish you for by not giving your body any sort of graciousness?' she chirps, fluttering above the expressionless, big, fat, ugly toad."

She sat up on the seat and opened the window to keep from falling asleep. The story stirred something in her and she listened closely now.

"'How unfortunate to have eyes that seem to want to flee from such a repulsive heap,' the beauty continued, even more annoyed at the big, fat, ugly toad's indifference. 'And what bad luck, too, to have your head in the mud when you walk. Me, it takes me less time

to touch the horizon than it takes for you to let out a single croak.'
In short, she's asking for trouble."

Obviously more interested in telling the young woman his story
than in driving, Kizito had slowed down considerably. He asked her
if she was following it, and she reassured him, not admitting that it
was all she was doing, and that she was worried, too, because she
wanted to figure out what the story refused to help her remember.

"The big, fat, ugly toad decides to react to this and croaks, 'My
beauty, give me a few seconds, and let's travel to whatever point
you'd like from here—to the horizon, if that's what you desire. Besides, I don't need to know the route. I'll follow the secret paths that
allow toads to go from one swamp to the next, and you, at each
swamp that you come across, you'll ask, "Toad, are you there?" And
I'll answer, "Are you following me?"'"

His voice grew soft and casual to utter the toad's words and
sharp and cutting when he played the swallow.

Still, despite the efforts of the storytelling driver and her own
interest, she fell asleep without hearing the end of the story and
without discovering what it suggested to her.

Seeing the scene in her mind again today should have amused
her, but she isn't in the mood.

When she woke up the next morning, she shook with fear when
she remembered she'd fallen asleep in a stranger's car. Fortunately,
although it took her some time to be certain of it, she really was at
the hotel. A card on the nightstand assured her of this: "Welcome
to the hotel. The director and his team will be glad to do everything to make your stay a pleasant one," the card commented to
her half-open eyes. The message was translated into English and,
on the back, various practical items of information were provided.
Relieved, she fell back asleep.

When she came down to the reception desk she found a note
Kizito had left for her, apologizing for having been so boring that
it had put her to sleep and saying he'd stop by that evening to collect his fare. Once again, the awareness that she'd let herself be in a
situation where she was at the mercy of a stranger's reliability made
her shiver. And then she felt something for Kizito that surpassed
gratitude.

SEVEN

114. As he grew older, Niko felt less and less like playing, and his daydreams were no longer an entertaining escape but rather the disconcerting echo of his loneliness. Being alone is one thing, but being aware of it is a problem, and being alone and aware of it is torture, he concluded. Niko had gone unnoticed for years since everyone was always too busy looking elsewhere. He only found company within himself.

115. The sole gaze under which Niko didn't feel he was transparent was Gaspard's. Without it ever being a conscious decision, Niko had become his son, his assistant, and his apprentice at the pottery-forge. He'd even been given tongs and a hammer so that he could replace his uncle should it be needed, a situation that occurred more and more frequently as the months went by, until the day when Niko realized he'd dropped out of school. Implicitly, it was understood that Gaspard would soon leave the forge in his hands to await death in a place that would suit his weakened body.

116. Everyone in the village took a stand for or against Niko as Gaspard's successor in the workshop. The rare ones who accepted it did so primarily out of loyalty to Gaspard, whose appreciation demanded their own. Besides, they'd add as an excuse, it would be better for Niko to inherit a responsibility that was at one and the same time by far the most taxing and harmless, too. Deep inside his workshop by day, and exhausted in his bed the rest of the time, Niko would no longer bother anyone. But far more numerous were those who were offended that Niko should occupy

such an important function. They found him much too eccentric and too much of a dilettante to be a reliable blacksmith and potter. But above all, how were they going to buy new tools and utensils from someone who couldn't talk and thus couldn't give them any of the recommendations that Gaspard offered? Wasn't it outlandish to use hoes, sickles, pots, or machetes engraved with the idiotic designs or phrases with which Niko had begun to embellish every piece that passed through his hands?

117. Unaware of any of this, Gaspard was proud of Niko, and the latter applied himself to his work in the forge, happy to be able to display his imagination elsewhere. He didn't just create functional objects. He wanted them to be as beautiful and interesting as possible. A pot that came from his workshop should be functional and beautiful, as well as interesting. To this end, and in addition to an impeccable finish, he engraved the objects with phrases. For example, on the blade of a machete: "The owner of this machete is the one who holds its handle." He'd place the phrase in such a way that it was impossible to read it while holding the hilt. On hoes he liked to state that the master of the method is inferior to the master of the thing. He inscribed sickles with the saying that the blade isn't fragile because it is thin. And on the pots he'd draw goats roasting men. He came up with many other ideas, and all of them ended up on one of the tools or utensils he produced.

118. Furious, people no longer bought anything from Niko, except for those on whom Gaspard still had enough influence that he could force them to come to his former workshop. Regardless of all this, Niko continued to churn out his articles, coating them with a product that prevented rusting and then storing them.

119. If an explorer were to get lost and reach the village, the first thing that would strike him would be the recurrent use of the name Niko in every conversation. Anywhere you'd go, people were constantly asking for news about him, asserting they'd run into him, insisting he was sick, and commenting on the phrases and designs he engraved on the objects he made. Undoubtedly, he would have noticed that, intermittently, it wasn't just the name Niko they brought up, but Niko the Monkey. In an attempt to understand, the traveler would head for the pottery-forge. Beneath a wide roof supported by several pillars, he would find a furnace and in front of it

an almost naked man, busy at work. For a moment he'd be capti-vated by the man, whose harmonious and powerful body was high-lighted by the reflections and shadows of the fire. He might well have wondered if this body, perfection incarnate, didn't glow on its own. Perhaps he envisioned it as imparting its radiance to the flames and not the other way around. Moving closer, he'd notice that in the most private area, Niko was astonishingly well equipped. Then Niko, who always knew when he was being observed, would turn around and, glad to have attracted someone's attention, would give the stranger a broad smile. The unexpected and hideous dis-parity of that smile would have squelched the intruder's burgeon-ing fascination as brutally as a snare squashes the little head of a trapped rat. The onlooker would feel as if he'd been struck by the lightning of disenchantment and disgust. And he'd have fled as far as he could, sure that in Niko he'd seen an angel and a demon, dazzling beauty and sickening ugliness, unbearably superimposed on each other.

120. His face and body personified harmony and grace. But when he smiled and revealed his teeth, as immense and ragged as they were in disarray, he seemed like a monkey to some and a devil to others. You had to be accustomed to them or warned be-forehand to be able to endure his smile without showing any sign of revulsion.

121. Niko knew it.

122. He also knew that this was why no woman would ever join him to seek her pleasure, and even less join him for life. Those who'd been initiated at the same time as he already had wives and even children. He remained alone and would certainly be so for-ever. Besides, he wondered, what is it two people do together? That was something about which he'd always been clueless. Not that he couldn't conceive of it in a general sense (in the realm of friend-ship or sexuality, he knew the possibilities were unlimited), but he just didn't worry about the issue. More specifically, then, he wasn't sure he had anything at all to do with the others. He didn't see any more combinations than there might be between a goat and a bicycle. That's precisely it: thinking about what he could have done with others or what others could have done with him seemed as inappropriate as wondering in what way a goat could relate to a

bicycle. Sure, the others were human beings just like he, but was that enough? What do two clouds do together? These are the terms in which he imagined his loneliness, the result of an incompatibility that was as incomprehensible and relentless as it was necessary. Given what he is, what bicycles, goats, and clouds are, what he is to the others and what they are to him, the question wasn't justified at all. If he asked it at all, it was only to reinforce the fact that it couldn't be answered.

123. Nevertheless, there was a mistake in this reasoning. A mistake or a lie. And deep within himself, Niko unsuccessfully persisted in stifling the small voice that accused him of exaggerating and even of falsifying. He wasn't as lonely as he told himself he was. Aside from Gaspard, who was always around, a few other individuals paid some attention to him. That attention was inconspicuous, for it was certainly not well looked upon to show any interest in Niko the Monkey, not to mention any affection or admiration. The lovely Hyacinthe, for example, with the long straight legs, always made sure she'd pass by the workshop whenever she was sent to run an errand.

124. Had Hyacinthe ever seen Niko smile? Is it possible that she'd been attracted to him, aware of the ghastly secret hidden behind his lips and knowing he was mute?

125. One day she dropped a jerrican with which she'd just drawn water from the well so that Niko, busy with something, would notice her. He'd come running to help put the container back on her head. He'd felt a warmth go through him as he approached her and again when he saw the swaying of her heavy chest as she walked away. He'd been careful not to smile at her so as not to frighten her. And that was all. After a while, he simply noticed that Hyacinthe no longer passed by. He observed it the way you notice that a given day is warmer or cooler than the previous one.

126. Does Niko's loneliness have anything to do with the fact that he feels unworthy of others? Or is he perhaps confined by the walls of his mutism—or else by the still higher ones his smile's disgrace has erected?

127. "That's where you're wrong," the small voice would sometimes mumble to him. "Whatever the explanations are that you're given, you're only lonely in appearance. And, fortunately, appear-

ance and reality are but an infinitesimal part of your existence. Think of what you have inside you! Is there loneliness inside you? On the contrary, isn't it constant anxiety, an overwhelming companionship, and even a warm smile that live inside there? Is what you perceive as loneliness not just an inability to accept that your development isn't actualized where that of normal people is, or of those who pretend to be normal?"

128. Goaded by the small voice, Niko then admitted that he wasn't entirely alone. His thoughts were inhabited by countless companions who were perhaps as worthy as the friends he didn't have and maybe never would have.

129. It's likely that the view he had of himself as a child, an adolescent, and then a solitary man was a fantasy in which he believed so strongly and for so long that he would end up finding fulfillment.

130. One day, seemingly engrossed in his work but actually bogged down in thoughts without any head or tail about what a chimpanzee could be doing with a tortoise, a tree in the forest with another tree, Niko has an accident. He's taking a large jug from the furnace and wants to put it down so it can cool off and finish drying. So he sets it on one of the upper struts of the storage space he has assembled for the articles he hardly ever sells anymore. It's a delicate operation because he must hold the object by its neck with the tongs and has to place it at a height of two grown men. The jug is heavy and threatens to slip every time he moves, but thanks to his patience Niko manages to put it down. However, before turning around, distracted by his thoughts on the possible connections—or not—between a butterfly and a fish or between a drowned person and a river's reed, he forgets to wedge it, and it falls on his head. He just has time to hear the jug roll and be aware that it's going to fall. Most of all he was afraid it would break, not that it would land on him. It was a double jolt: first that of the jug against his skull, and then that of his body against the ground, buckling like a marionette whose strings have suddenly been cut. He even had time to think that the jug, too, had suffered two shocks: the irrelevant one against his head and the deadly one against the ground.

131. When he opened his eyes again, he wondered how long he had been down on the ground. It was still bright daylight; he

couldn't have been unconscious for more than a few hours, he assured himself, unless he'd fallen asleep for one or several days. He looked to see if the fire in the furnace was still lit. It was not, but the ashes were still smoking. It didn't help him estimate how long he'd been out. The fire died very quickly when it wasn't tended, and the ash could smoke for more than a week, depending on the amount of smoldering charcoal.

132. If he'd relied on what was going on inside his head during this time, he would insist he'd slept for an eternity. Were he to be more specific, he would compare that eternity to the stealth of lightning whose disappearance from the sky is as rapid as the violence with which it rips the heavens apart.

133. The first thing that appears is the worried and disquieting face of the old woman, alone on a barren, arid plain. She'd seen him, was coming towards him, calling him her son. Then, as usual, in the time it took to reach him she'd become a young girl of heartrending beauty who assured him of her love and begged him to follow her. For the first time in all these years, he was receptive to these two women. He looked at the first one the way he might have looked at his mother. As the second one came close, he felt the same warmth that had run through him when he was close to Hyacinthe. In his dream, also for the first time, he accepted the young girl's invitation and trailed her scent instead of following her at a distance.

134. They walk for a long time until they come to a small pirogue floating quietly on a thick lava flow. Impassioned by his companion's sad gaze, Niko doesn't spare himself and paddles energetically against the current to the source of the lava river, which is nothing other than the workshop's furnace. A rejuvenated Gaspard is waiting for him. He resembles the one whose every aspect had so fascinated Niko a few years earlier, but has a piercing look besides. His eyes are a combination of cat and serpent. The young girl who he's sure had come with him is now nowhere to be seen. Niko wants to ask where she went but all that comes from his mouth is bleating, instantly imitated by a mocking Gaspard. "Baa!" he repeats until he bursts into derisive laughter that resounds endlessly between Niko's ears. At that moment, a suffocating fear rises in Niko, but he doesn't try to escape it. Strangely, the anxiety makes him want to smile, and so he does. He's smiling even as he sees Gaspard's tongs move

toward him, at the level of his neck, lift him up, and hold him suspended above the furnace. The thundering laughter still reverberates in every part of Niko's body, and then, gradually, his trembling becomes intolerable. He feels his skin tighten, and his whole body dilates and finally explodes. Each one of his pieces, dispersing in the air, prevails with complete and autonomous consciousness. The multiplication of his gaze, his sensitivity, and his will stuns him. A myriad minuscule Nikos are whirling through the workshop, and each of these confettis sees, feels, and comments on the incredible scene in which he is both spectator and actor.

135. "Dear companion, at the beginning of the story there was a word of warning to you that it might be uncomfortable for those who, among other things, confuse logic and meaning and need their assimilation in order to move ahead. Nothing of what's just been told holds up. Even a mind loosened by a belief in magic or a being sensitive to naïveté might find it difficult to connect with certain elements. In any event, it seemed so to me, and I haven't managed to keep approaching Niko other than by accepting that his story, illogical though it be, is not that outrageous. If you have the same problem and if you don't have a better idea to grasp onto, I invite you to make the distinction between logic and meaning your own. Perhaps that will help you as much as it does me."

*   *   *

When she had the interview with the Foundation, it was understood that a partnership with other financial backers was yet to be arranged. Nevertheless, unable to go along at their pace, she decided to anticipate the resolution of the financial setup by going on-site and launching what she could. The decision wasn't the result of any real consideration but a way of protecting herself from her impatience.

Once there, she realized that without funds and without being covered by the Foundation, which hadn't authorized her to introduce herself in its name, there wasn't very much she could do. In fact, there wasn't anything she could do. The first week she phoned every day to express her concern about the slow pace at which things were proceeding and her hope that the means, her reason for leaving, would soon be in her hands. Invariably, the voice would merely point out two things to her. In the first place, without a letter that contained the mission statement, itself dependent on the funds being made available, she ought not to forget she couldn't introduce herself and act except in her own name. And, secondly, they were with her.

When she called for the thirteenth time, a new point was added to the two ritual observations. Thirdly, the voice on the other end of the line said, she shouldn't forget that she'd departed without the Foundation's endorsement. The voice hadn't bothered to bring the thought to its obvious completion: the Foundation wasn't responsible for her impatience nor for the deadlock she'd caused herself, and would she please be so good as to stop pestering them with all that might imply? Those words, even in the abstraction of a memory, remained very painful. She heard them as a betrayal and thereafter saw herself alone with her project *In Memory of . . .*

Forced to hold off, but unwilling to add boredom to her waiting period, she resolved to visit the country, which seemed like a fine way of spending the time she was obliged to fill.

On impulse she asked Kizito to be her guide on this adventure. Thanks to the hotel receptionist, who turned out to be a relative of his, she found him. He didn't hesitate for a moment to accept her invitation; he was actually impressed, as if he'd been expecting it. Finally, a new route that would allow him to make the most of his talents as driver, guide, storyteller, mechanic, and cook. When he offered her these details she wondered if she'd made the right choice, but Kizito was already planning the program. He wanted to take her to see the gorillas, of course, or rather drop her off at a place where she could go see them, for these animals didn't inspire any confidence in him. "I should also take you to visit the Island of Nez. I expect you've heard about it already. That's the island they say was born a very long time ago when travelers wandering around the lake were supposed to have thrown stones into it." He no longer knew what the importance of this gesture had been, he explained, but in the end the stones tossed into the water grew into such an immense pile that it protruded above the lake and formed the island. "The most astounding thing," he clarified, "is that this gigantic cairn took the shape of a nose instead of looking like a normal heap of stones. The result is that travelers today no longer throw anything in to keep it from getting still larger. They're happy to explain that the island is nothing but the replica of their own noses. As incredible as it may seem, it has resulted in bloody arguments, and hundreds of thousands of people have even been massacred." Finally, he promised her he'd show her the national brewery, the continent's largest one, the forest of the royal drums, the animal reserve, and many other things.

She had to bow to the fact that he hadn't understood. He saw her as a tourist and not as someone who was coming home after a long absence and wanted nothing more than to bring back to life everything that was congealed in her memory. At that moment she didn't bother to disappoint him by explaining that none of it held much interest for her, that she hadn't come to see landscapes and animals, but people. If that was what she had wanted to see, she could just as easily have stayed in Paris and taken a trip to the Vincennes Zoo or gone to the Jardin d'Acclimatation or, for that matter, watched a documentary on one of those special channels.

Would he have understood if she'd told him that she specifically wanted to hear the sounds, smell the scents, taste the flavors that had cradled her childhood? Wouldn't he have laughed in her face if she'd admitted that, more than anything else, she wanted to find the place where the begonias grew and ask someone there whether anyone remembered a little girl who answered to the name Isaro twenty-five years ago? Would he have agreed to drive her if she'd divulged that she wanted to go to the graves of her people and, should none exist, make one herself, enshroud it with her tears, and place a cross on it? She promised herself she'd bring up those questions later when they knew each other better.

Before setting out on the trip and not knowing whether she'd find any post office along the way, resolved at last to take the step, she finally sent a letter to her parents. She remembers every word of this message as if they were engraved in her:

"Dear Papa, dear Mama," she began. She wanted to call them this again and not by their first names as she'd started doing once she'd left for Paris. "I have fled from you and hated you these past few years but realize now that I only fled from, and hated, myself. Too cowardly to admit it, I saw you as the source of this dejection even though you were doing your utmost to alleviate it. I don't feel I have the right to ask for forgiveness, but I think it and I hope you still have a little patience left for me to accept my return to reason, to life and, consequently, to you." She'd almost stopped there but added: "Nevertheless, there is one thing for which I think I was right to blame you and that is that you never told me anything of what had happened, of the events that led you to take me in, basically, of who I am." She clarified it was no excuse for her behavior towards them but that perhaps it would let them understand the place from where it had sprung. Before closing the envelope she realized she almost forgot to mention she'd gone back to her country and that this was from where she was writing. She enclosed a copy of her project presentation to give them an idea of what she was doing here. As she was about to slip the envelope in the mailbox, she held on to it for a second. The letter's contents seemed to fall short of everything she'd wanted to say to them. She let go of it when it occurred to her that a whole book wouldn't have been enough, that nothing would ever be enough.

EIGHT

136. Niko's dream goes beyond the scattering of his body. That vision is just the beginning of a whole series of still more incredible experiences.

137. In his dream, all the pieces land in one of the large containers stored on the shelves of the workshop and come together again to shape a new Niko. His skin is firmer, his shoulders broader, his heart more serene, his face more assured—and, he can feel it, his eyes now shine as if set with a diamond focusing its power. He has the feeling of being a lighter, a more robust, and a more self-confident version than the one he was before. Gaspard is no longer present when he comes out of the jar. The workshop is silent. The silence seems to express awe for this new being. He is respected for the first time. Alone, but respected. The solitude worthy of a lion or a gorilla and not the miserable loneliness of the hyena. Alone because no one dares to come near him and not because no one wants to come near him.

138. Perhaps I am able to speak, he tells himself without trying. He's too afraid it might be true or that it might not. The two options seem equally terrifying to him, and he tells himself that in not attempting to speak, not even attempting to be disappointed or embarrassed by a new possibility it's more reasonable not to risk getting all mixed up. Speech is the only limitation to his otherwise uncontainable power.

139. In the vision to which he abandons himself under the blow of the pot, Niko has uncontrollable strength. When he thinks he's

taking a simple step, his new strength deludes him, and he leaps higher than the clouds. Up there he bursts into the middle of an undeniable herd of white goats and sheep. Noticing his astonishment, a splendid male goat with horns and a bushy beard moves away from the herd, comes toward him, and bleats, "Surely you didn't really expect clouds to be anything other than an immense herd of white goats and sheep? Seen from a distance it looks just like a clustered mass that then separates, runs off or relaxes in the middle of the sky, but not so, my friend, not so!"

Niko isn't surprised by what he sees and hears. To demonstrate his interest and attention he sits down. The goat continues, "Ah, yes, my friend, people have ideas about everything, but if they knew how far from the truth they are, they'd die with shame. Look at the rain, for example: some believe it comes from the clouds, which are supposed to be a sort of immense sponge suspended in the air. What a ludicrous idea! In reality, the rain falls from much higher up. The gods have allocated a certain amount of it, which has been crossing the world since the beginning of time."

The goat notices Niko's baffled gaze and grows indignant. "Don't tell me that you, too, imagine the Earth as a pancake hanging by itself in the middle of nothing! No, Niko! Not that! Not you!"

Niko can't remember having introduced himself.

"In truth," the goat goes on, "the world you know is just a small part of a multitude of worlds overlapping each other in the shape of a spiral that itself forms a crown. Are you following me? No? Imagine a spiral, or rather, let's say, a cord you've wound around a stick and that stays in place there. Well then, tell yourself that this cord, which is actually a collage of bits of cord—the worlds—that you take this cord and make it into a loop. Are you with me or not?"

"It's not easy, but I'm trying," Niko answers by nodding.

"Well then," the goat continues, who was nothing if not talkative, "our world is only a part, one floor, of this looped spiral, and the water that falls on it—I'm talking about our world—well, the water that falls on it during the rainy season comes from higher up and in turn is poured out over the next world. It comes back a year later during the rainy season when it has completed the cycle of the spiral of worlds."

What the goat interprets as incomprehension on Niko's face is actually surprise. Niko remembers already having had this idea of superimposing worlds. It was the explanation he'd given of the cave that, as he and his fantasy saw it, could only be the door that gave you access from our world to the next.

"Fine, it looks like meteorology isn't your strong point," the goat fires at him, giving him a well-meaning shove.

Then he apologizes for having to join the herd again and slips away. Niko is dazed for a moment. One part of him tries to recall that it's only a vision caused by the blow he'd received, but the other part accepts it without any hesitation.

140. Remembering he's arrived there by accident, Niko comes back down. But once again he forgets the force that carries him since he's been divided into bits and reconstructed, and he leaps wildly. Then, instead of simply landing on solid ground, Niko burrows deep into the ground. He stops in a cave where something like birds are whirling around, occasionally colliding with him. The darkness doesn't allow him to see what kind of birds he's dealing with. He only hears wings flapping, sharp cries, and one of their breaths in passing. He wonders how they've managed to land in such a place and thrive here. What do they look like? For some reason, which he doesn't try to explain, he thinks of them as crows.

141. After quite a while, during which he finds nothing to confirm or weaken his assumption, the agitation subsides. In front of him only a shimmer is left, like stars in a clear sky, which he imagines to be eyes. All of a sudden a deep voice emerges:

"You know . . ." it says.

While he's felt no embarrassment at all until now, Niko gulps noisily. He doesn't know whether these words are an affirmation, a question, or the beginning of a commentary the rest of which the voice has forgotten.

"You know why you're here, I hope?" the voice remarks, now seeming closer.

He shakes his head, no. "Do you see me?" he would like to have asked if he were able.

"It's been years since we've been asking for a messenger. It's a pity you're only now arriving. We didn't want to keep the knowledge of what will soon be happening to ourselves," the voice goes on, immediately protracted by a torrent of commentary from all sides.

"No, we can't keep that to ourselves!"

"That's for sure. It's much too awful."

"But is there still time to tell them?"

"It's too serious!"

"Dreadful, you mean!"

"Why did it take him so long to get here? That's not very responsible, if I may say so."

"They should at least be informed."

"I've already told you that it serves no purpose, and I'm sticking to my guns."

"Poor things, half of them will end up butchered like cattle . . ."

"Oh, no! We said we wouldn't go into detail!"

"If only it could still serve a purpose."

"How can they tell?"

"It's their own fault. All they had to do was hear our calls!"

"Yes, but without any detail how do you expect them to understand?"

"Blood will flow, unprecedented amounts of blood . . ."

"What good, then, is it to warn them if the game is up?"

"There you have it: forewarned is forearmed!"

"Do you think the blood will actually flow all the way here?"

"Are you sure he's the one we should tell all this to?"

"Don't make me laugh!"

"Yes?"

"Or not . . ."

"We'll have to move then?"

"Me, in their place, I'd prepare myself to be on the good side when the moment comes."

"You said half of them, but I see a whole lot more than that."

"And don't make any mistake, in some cases being spineless or cruel is just as tempting as being brave or good."

"How awful!"

"He's so little; I find it hard to believe they'd choose him."

"And to say that at this very moment they're sowing the seeds whose shoots will be drowned in blood."

"By the killers, you mean?"

"Well, I think it'll be more than that. More dead, I mean . . ."

"They couldn't have come up with a hero with a head and especially a size less ridiculous than that?"

"But are we sure about it?"

"That's really rubbish! Size has nothing to do with it."

"And to top it off, it's got a machete, too . . ."

"And letting their cattle graze without worrying."

"All we're doing now is wasting what little time they've got left to live a normal life."

"This really is rubbish; in my time we never interfered in the business of humans."

"But what about us? Is there anything we can do?"

"At any rate he's not a kid!"

"Let's be specific, anyhow: there will be firearms as well. And besides, it won't be half, it'll be a third."

"Telling them that now is really very much too late."

"Stop, please, no details, it's sickening."

"I agree, it's too late now."

"It's true that, under certain circumstances, killing someone or leaving him to die is just as tempting as saving him."

"You can say what you want, but I don't approve of this kind of intervention in the business affairs of humans! Let that be clearly understood."

"They'll realize that soon enough, unfortunately."

"Who wants to add to it?"

"Stop with all your thoroughness, for heaven's sake, or we might come to blows yet. It's sad enough knowing it's going to happen. We don't need to add to it."

"Even one third is too many!"

And so on, until it became impossible to recognize a single word. After this lengthy cacophony that made his head spin, the solemn voice that had started it off cuts through; silence returns.

"I think you understand the basics," it says before the noise smothers it again. Niko realized he no longer needed to stay there.

142. Being careful to control his impulse this time, Niko returns to the surface. Despite the inexhaustible enthusiasm that carries him, he feels devoid of any thought, of any emotion.

143. He passes through the same devastated landscape as before. The little pirogue is where he'd left it. He gets in and goes down the lava stream. He notices that the trip is easier now. Is it because the current is helping him? Is it because he's alone in the boat? Is it because the force that's overtaken him numbs him to the effort? As usual, he's happy just to ask questions.

144. One of the rare times that his father talked to him directly, he'd told him to always be wary of answers. "Distrust any answers," he'd warned him. "Always stay away from people who have answers and flee from those who, before they offer the responses they present as being easy, explain that all questions are, after all, simple. No question is simple, my son, and so no answer can be simple, either." He remembers these words as if he'd just heard them. It was the only time his father ever called him "my son." Perhaps his father spoke so little because this phrase summarized everything he had to tell him. Perhaps he'd thought of this advice before and then couldn't find anything further to add to it. That's what Niko is contemplating while, in his dream, he quietly paddles down a stream of lava.

145. When he glimpses a figure in the distance, he has no doubts about its identity.

146. The elegance of each of her gestures surprises him as if he'd never seen the woman before. Without waiting for him to set foot on firm soil, she turns around and moves away. He understands he is to follow her. He slinks behind her, as when he came, in utter silence.

147. In silence they walk on, for a long time. After a while a tree of staggering height rises before them, whose roots, in their effort to bolster it, seem as if they must descend to hell itself. Its foliage, with unexpected exuberance for this region, attracts Niko's curiosity; he moves closer. "It's the tree of life," says the girl. "It grows here on our path so you will consult it. Then your spell will come to an end." Niko is barely listening to what she's saying, fascinated both by the sadness in her voice and the overabundant foliage. Nevertheless, he does notice her emphasis on the word "spell." "Each leaf represents a person, and every time a human being is born a new leaf grows, and every time a human being dies one falls off. Every time a new work generates progress in respect between humans or between humans, animals, and nature, a new fruit grows." Sud-

denly borne upward by these words, Niko rises into the air and approaches the leaves. There is very little fruit. "Soon the tree will be almost bare," the girl adds. Niko can see that she's right. On each of the leaves he reads a name, two dates, and the mention of a few milestones. One leaf bears the name of Fulgence Uwijoro. Besides the dates of his birth and death, it says: "Studied letters, teacher, diabetic, married to Beata Nyiringoma, four children, killer, life sentence." Poor man, he thinks. What a sad career! Out of curiosity he looks for his own leaf. He finds Gaspard Uzubitse's where, in addition to the dates, he reads: "Blacksmith-potter, married to Elizabeth Munyaneza, three children and one adopted son, alcoholic, died of fatigue." He keeps looking for his leaf but finds only those of other people, unfamiliar ones, acquaintances, or members of his family.

Following the dates, his father's leaf states: "Roger Karinzi, farmer, married to Eugenie Isaro who died in childbirth, one child; united in marriage with Maria Uwase, two children. Killed by his son." Niko jumps with a start. Anguish pours in heavy drops beneath his arms. "Before long there will be more leaves on the ground than on the tree," the girl whispers to him. "In any case, that's what the dates on the leaves reveal. Most of the dates of their deaths are the same or very close together." It seems the girl is weeping as she speaks, but when he turns around no one is there anymore. "Killed by his son." The phrase sets off such fierce anxiety in him that it surpasses the dream. He is truly in agony and wakes up.

148. When he opens his eyes he has no idea how long he's been unconscious on the ground. He's relieved. Everything that upset him was only a nightmare.

149. But the pain is still there, in his chest, in his belly, and in his head. And then there's that phrase: "killed by his son." His father had only one son. Himself. From his second marriage he had just two daughters.

150. For an instant he tries to see all these thoughts as pure crap. How can so many people disappear at the same time? What insanity can justify and accomplish such a thing? How could he have ended up killing his own father? He doesn't even think about him enough for him to be part of his regular reflections, so why would he have killed him? Why should two strangers kill each other? Pure crap!

151. If anyone, Hyacinthe for instance, had passed by the workshop at that moment, she wouldn't have dared come closer and would have called for help. Indeed, without being aware of it, Niko looks like a hanged person just cut down from the rope. The kind of face you use to threaten children with when they grumble about going to sleep. But nobody passed by—not Hyacinthe, not anyone else—and for a long time Niko stayed flat on the ground before he noticed that the sounds he was hearing had a strange, disquieting color.

152. Things had changed a lot since he'd lost consciousness.

*   *   *

The typed letter had been sent from Paris a few days earlier.

She found it upon her return. Her travels had left her with the impression of an "overloaded" experience. The word may seem inappropriate but it came to her naturally the first time she tried to describe what she'd just come to know. Was it this journey that gave birth to the melancholy with which she stands motionless in front of the window, to the point of making you wonder at times whether she's actually alive?

"*Mademoiselle,*

After newly analyzing your project titled In Memory of . . . *and taking into account the elements you provided in writing and in the interview, the Foundation regretfully announces that it is withdrawing its commitment to you. Various components that could only recently be assessed have come together to lead to this decision.*

We are aware of the inconvenience this outcome represents for you, and we beg you to accept our apologies. In the end, your idea, if it is to become a reality, which we do not doubt, will find the necessary support. Be that as it may, we encourage you to continue.

Mademoiselle, on behalf of the Foundation and its Grants Committee, I am

Sincerely yours . . ."

Added was an illegible signature concealing the identity of the individual who had taken it upon himself to deal with this matter.

She was momentarily paralyzed by contradictory feelings, stunned in front of the hotel's reception desk long enough for Kizito, who was parking the car, to return and find her in the same position. "What's the matter, dear girl?" he inquired, awkwardly imitating the Parisian accent she'd spent a good bit of the trip teaching him. She shook her head, as if awakening, and assured him it wasn't anything dramatic. Kizito, who'd come to know her during the past few weeks, was worried. Her calm façades were rarely a good omen. He persisted and she told him everything, from the very beginning. He already knew snatches of the story: the radio that screamed instead of turning off, her studies dropped, the idea of the project, her nomination for the grant, her locking herself in, the death, the interview for the grant, the Foundation's basic agreement, her impatience that had brought her here before she'd received the go-ahead, and this letter, every word of which seemed to be a mockery intended to grind up her entrails. He took her in his arms long enough for her to rail against those who'd betrayed her, weep, and pull herself together again. She decided to take at least one line of this missive seriously, the one that encouraged her not to abandon her project. Kizito assured her of his support. Besides, she could move in with him and do whatever she wanted while he was at work. She accepted and made the move immediately.

During the trip, without any real discussion, their relationship had changed. The first day they found lodging that she would never have entered had she been alone. That night Kizito, who was supposed to sleep in an adjoining room, insisted on coming to tell her the end of the story of the toad and the swallow. She tried to make him understand that it could wait, they could keep it for the next day's drive. For reasons she's forgotten, he'd made it seem logical that it wasn't possible. He had to tell her right away. He kept on teasing her and then asked what she'd give him if he stopped talking. She told him she'd give him whatever he wanted on the condition he'd be quiet. "Checkmate," he muttered as he came toward her on tiptoe, mimicking exaggerated caution. He wanted to spend the night with her—this night and every other night. He didn't go back to his room, and from then on they shared their bed and introduced themselves as a couple.

She noticed he was less talkative and less agitated thereafter. So there was no reason for her not to love him.

NINE

153. Getting up at last, recovered from his blackout, Niko had the odd sensation that the air had changed; it entered his nostrils with greater difficulty and blocked his lungs like a gooey liquid. Besides being heavy, the air seemed noisier to him. A combination of songs, speeches, cries, explosions, and prayers filled his ears. All the stages of his dream, nightmare or delirium, were piling up inside his head: the old woman, the young girl, the scattering of his body, the goat, the story of the clouds, the cave and the crows, the tree of life. Then there was the pain in his head as well, and the fatigue that weighed each part of his body down to the point where he had the impression it was a leaden skeleton that kept him upright.

154. As he chases away his drowsiness with yawns and stretches, he hears cries and then sees Hyacinthe running past the workshop. She throws him a panic-stricken look but doesn't stop. A group of men is in pursuit, machetes and clubs in hand. Without thinking about what he's doing, Niko drops a jar, and the noise catches the attention of the group that stops and now heads in his direction.

"Let her run," one of the men lashes out, visibly out of breath. "She won't get very far in any case. If we don't find her later others will take care of it."

Niko pretends he hasn't seen them and gathers up the pieces of the jar.

"Is that Niko the joker or am I dreaming?" the man goes on. "They're looking for you everywhere, Niko the Monkey."

"Why were you hiding?" another voice continues.

"You can answer at least, you idiot. Such insolence!" yells the one who appears to be the leader, pointing his weapon at him.

"He's mute," corrects one of the men, whom Niko thinks he's seen before, maybe at school.

Alphonse, he remembers. At the same time, as if the tree of life in his dream had taken the place of his brain, he sees the leaf again, whose dates had been missing: "Alphonse Munyejabo, scientific studies, merchant, married to Isabelle Uwimana, no children, killer, life imprisonment."

"Why are you hiding?"

"Does anyone know this man?" the leader barks.

No one responds, not even Alphonse. Why are the others whom he recognizes pretending never to have seen him before? How can they be looking for him without knowing who he is? Someone whispers something in the leader's ear.

"Come with us!" they shout at him.

155. He hears them talking about him. The leader, who apparently is not from the region, asks whether he is really mute. They all confirm it.

"As mute as a grave, and always has been," corroborates Alphonse, who seems to have found his memory again.

"Fine. And is he with us or not? If not, we don't need to drag him along. We'll make him a head shorter right here and that'll be that."

"His father is with us, but his mother, who's been dead a long time, was a barbarian," Alphonse continues.

"I wouldn't be so sure about his father, because he did remarry another mole. Is a brother who marries a mole, even when life gives him another chance to correct his choice, still one of us?"

"Certainly not," the leader cuts in. "Besides, we'll go find him, and his son will have to cut him down himself if he wants to be one of us. That'll be the sign of his goodwill. Otherwise we'll kill them both."

156. The wasteland where he'd spent so much time playing when he was small is a place of unusual and unsettling bustle. He wonders where all these people could be coming from. As he comes closer he notes that the swarm isn't as chaotic as it seems. People chained together like him are sitting in the middle of the field.

Mutilated corpses are piled up in the back. Men carrying all kinds of weapons are circulating around and between these two groups. Most of them carry machetes, but some also have clubs, lances, bows, sickles, pitchforks, and scissors—anything that can be used to strike, stab, or slash. Some of the men, generally those who are giving the orders, have firearms. Then they tell him to sit with those who've been gagged. He rushes over and struggles to become as invisible as he can, for in this situation it seems to him that being noticed is the worst possible thing. If he could have fled, become truly invisible, or even died without any pain, he would have done so. Something tells him it's the one and final moment that he'll be able to imagine these options. Soon it will be too late.

157. Besides breathe, tremble, and blink his lowered eyes, the only thing he can do without any risk is listen.

"The ones over there still need to be finished off, and quickly."

"We'll have to put the others somewhere else because they'll start to reek soon. Or else we'll have to hold our meetings in a different place."

"We'd better finish off the next group farther down."

"What are we waiting for? We're falling behind."

"They're somewhat on our side, so we should give them the opportunity to prove themselves. And it will give the men a chance to rest."

"There's no time. All we have to do is finish them all off, and God will sort out the rest."

Other snatches of dialogue reach him, and every one of them indicates that his life is hanging above a chasm by a thin string that an unexpected breeze could break in an instant. The morning flows by.

158. When the group that brought him here returns, flanking new people all tied together, among whom he thinks he sees Hyacinthe, things begin to pick up speed.

159. There are about thirty of those who must prove themselves. For a brief moment he remains bewildered, his brain tangled up inside his cranium like the legs of a child on a bicycle hurtling too fast down a slope.

160. "You over there! Look here, the situation is simple, so simple that theoretically you won't even need to think about it. We have

no way of knowing whether you're on our side or not. If you want to demonstrate that you're with us, you'll have to participate in our work, starting right now. Otherwise you'll be executed on the spot. To make things easier, we've brought you the barbarians to be eliminated. You won't need to flush them out, chase them down, or attack them in the turmoil. If you give us solid proof, you can come and hunt with us." The man with the Kalashnikov speaks solemnly, as if he were introducing an athletic competition.

161. One of Gaspard's sons is the first to be called before the throng. Absorbed by his fear, Niko hadn't seen him, and the reverse was probably true as well. The scene, to be repeated some thirty times, lines up three individuals. The one who must die is kneeling in front, with his back to the crowd. Behind the first person stands the one who has to prove himself. The second individual is untied and must choose a weapon: a machete, a club—anything but a rifle. The third person aims at the second one with a gun or a Kalashnikov. The latter counts backward starting at three. If the second one hasn't struck the person kneeling before zero is reached, the third man kills them both.

162. Gaspard's son's name is Anastase. An old woman is on her knees before him. She is weeping; he is shaking.

163. Three, two, one. He hesitates. Two shots. The bodies of Anastase and the old woman are hauled off to the pile with the other corpses.

164. "Next!" they shout. "You there!" Niko hesitates, pretending not to hear they're summoning him, but then he remembers what that may cost. So he takes the few steps that will bring the victim within his reach. In this lapse of time, all kinds of ideas go through his head: run and get a bullet in his back, explain that he cannot do it and get a bullet between the eyes. In any event, after they kill him they'll kill the one who obviously must die, they'll throw both their corpses on top of the others, and they'll shout, "Next!"

165. What should one do when resistance, even through the sacrifice of oneself, will not save anything or anyone? Does the hand of the one who kills this way have any other motive for killing besides self-preservation? Why, at this moment, is Niko incapable of doing what he was so sure he'd do just a few minutes before?

166. The man prostrated before him has the same stoutness as his father, the same baldness, too. He's restless and even stands up to beg for mercy from the man with the gun. Niko lowers his head and closes his eyes as he awaits the countdown. The man has the same voice as his father, but that doesn't mean anything, he convinces himself. He closes his eyes very tightly in an attempt not to hear the man say to him with confidence and assurance: "You can't do this to me. I'm sure you won't do it."

167. When Niko hears "three" he opens his eyes and focuses all his attention on the neck that's not his father's but belongs to some man or animal from somewhere else. Everything in him converges to persuade him of this. The man behind him loads his weapon. Niko would like to yell "Lower your head!" at the man when from behind him he hears "two." He's chosen a club so as not to have to see the blood. "One." He strikes with all his might, and the man who resembles his father slumps down, face against the ground, without any sound other than that of the club crushing his skull. The gathering applauds. He knows most of the faces. Careful not to leave any doubt of his proof and commitment, Niko even gives a little half-smile. The man behind him has put his weapon down to shake his hand and adds that this club belongs to him. "From now on it will be your work tool. That was good. Efficient. We need people like you." Niko's only concern is to avoid seeing the corpse they're now pushing to the side.

168. Had he just killed his father? Niko convinced himself that he didn't know and that in the end it didn't matter. The only thing that left its mark on him right then was that when he had been asked to bend his head, the man had obeyed. Why does the victim obey his executioner when he knows there's no earthly way to escape? This absorbs him the whole time it takes to prepare for the next execution. Using him as their model, those who follow don't hesitate to choose their camp.

169. Why did the man obey him when he knew he was going to die anyway? Perhaps, he thinks, it was a matter of dying politely and obediently, attitudes to which he must have attached great importance. Don't they say that it's in the face of death that we reveal the most profound characteristics of our temperament? He must have been a polite and obedient man, he repeats to himself, noting

that this had never been one of the strong points of his father, who therefore couldn't have been the man he killed. Another thought comes to him. When a victim follows the instructions given, it may be a question of leaving all the guilt to the executioner, a way of saying, "You have no reason whatsoever to kill me, and I won't give you any possible pretext for it by disobeying or struggling with you." Obeying so as to leave the executioner alone with his crime to the very end. Unless, until the final moment and in spite of the first execution, the man thought that complying could save him. Obedience as a sign of the implacability of hope, the last entrenchment in desperate situations. That's what animals most definitely don't have, since as soon as they feel even the most distant threat they put all their energy into escape. Can you say, then, he continues, that the main difference between humans and animals lies in their attitude toward death? Humans hope, even when death is certain, while animals have doubts even when they're in absolute safety.

170. He keeps his eyes closed while the executions are carried out in front of him, surrendering to a relentless self-interrogation. Is cruelty born from a kind of instinct that tells you that any form of rebellion will cost you your own life and changes nothing in the situation against which you rebel? Does the instinct of survival justify killing? Is it better to die so as not to kill the other, who must die no matter what? Fragments from his reading in the *bimo* come back to him. The advice of a certain Jesus and of someone by the name of Kant, he remembers. What would they have done in the same situation? And then there's that phrase he can't get out of his mind: "Killed by his son." Did he just kill his father?

171. With time, insensitivity flowed into him like cement and set in his face. Every one of his expressions faded away, reduced to a kind of perfect mask. A mask on which a gifted sculptor might have chiseled the illusion of human skin, rendering the movement of the eyes, the articulation of the jaw.

172. When the work at the wasteland was done, Niko brought the men he now commanded to his workshop. They had to have new machetes and clubs before they could carry out their task. "The owner of this machete is he who holds its handle," one of them read, remarking how funny that phrase and its position on the handle

were. "I have better ones than that!" Niko seemed to be saying when he gave them the rest of the equipment. Even those villagers who only yesterday found them insufferable were now laughing out loud.

Armed to the hilt, the group decided they needed a name. The Worry-Free, the Lions, the Committed, the Ninjas, the Willful, the Leopards. Suggestions rang out. Pointing to the ones who had proposed it, Niko opted for the Intentionally Enraged. And the group was ready to begin the hunt, singing their name to a tune they all knew.

173. What happened next surpasses any horror or cruelty that even the most depraved mind might picture. Niko's group murdered as many people as it could, at first following the orders and signals of the leaders, and then simply in competition with each other—"I must have killed at least twenty today, and you?"—and, finally, out of habit. When the job began to feel monotonous to them, it was no longer a matter of just numbers of victims, but also how they were executed: sliced to pieces, buried after being stoned nearly to death, strung up head down, and countless other ways. In the evening, to celebrate or to forget the day's accomplishments, beer and banana wine flowed, and unlimited amounts of skewered meat and grilled corn were consumed until deep into the night. They had to recuperate from today and be fortified for tomorrow.

174. One of those evenings, Gaspard died after drinking too much. Since he was no longer working at the forge, drinking had become his sole activity. As he jokingly told those around him, he was trying to quench the thirst of a lifetime in the unbearable heat of his workshop. When his uncle suddenly collapsed in his chair, Niko was the only one who worried, leaving food and drink behind to go to his side. He realized that he was gone, closed his eyes, and lugged the body outside. He felt the kind of sorrow he might have felt for the death of his father, had the latter acted like one. He never heard anyone speak of Gaspard again.

175. How long had this been going on? How many people was he killing? Since the first man he slayed, the man who could not have been his father, he no longer experienced death as a specific event. Even his sorrow over Gaspard's death was short-lived. Everything that follows is but the sequel of that first act, a confused and

grueling flood. Occasionally, one sentence comes back to him: "In certain cases, being cruel is as tempting as being good." At the time he hadn't understood that temptation is the enticement of security. He becomes conscious of the fact that *in certain cases* the choice doesn't lie between accepting and refusing horror, collaborating in it or distancing oneself from it, but between standing on the side of those who commit the horror or on the side of those who suffer it. Two options between which one *must* choose.

176. Immersed in the killings, Niko feels fine. Up to a point, he's actually happy. For the first time in his life he's part of a community, is respected, and feels unlimited power. Being mute contributes to imposing his authority over the Intentionally Enraged, and beyond. His men follow his orders to the letter, and the discussions that slow down the work of the other groups never take place in his. In the beginning someone tried to protest his method, arguing that the work had to be done, of course, but that they didn't need to go about it with such zeal. After all, the man had advocated, we have nothing against these barbarians who've been our neighbors and friends for ages. Niko killed him with one blow of his club to the forehead and, from that day on, nobody made any further comment on the way he led his group.

177. But, obviously, killings don't go on forever. There comes a day when there's no one left to kill. The routine comes to a halt and, with it, the illusion to which Niko had been clinging ever since the day he'd slaughtered the man who had his father's features.

178. Is a killer just a killer at the exact moment of the murder? How do you punish those who, like Niko, have killed to the point of not being able to count the number of their victims? What expectations does one have from such punishment?

179. When there's no one left to kill, life takes its time returning to normal. First the bodies, scattered all over the place, have to be buried. And the very ones who, only yesterday, were clubbing other people senseless the way you flatten a sorghum field, are now astonished to find corpses everywhere: in trees, streets, rivers, on the furniture in homes, in churches, everywhere. Unceremonious burials. The only thing that matters is disposing of the stench. Burying quickly, not out of respect for the dead, but to allow the killers and their accomplices to forget acts they had and hadn't committed.

That, at least, in the silence of his reflections, is what Niko admits from the very start as being his primary motivation. If there's no further proof that people have died, everyone can act as if nothing ever happened and—who knows?—maybe even be convinced of it in the end.

180. Erasure followed by oblivion promptly became a reality. No one spoke of, or alluded to, the massacres. In a way, those who had died had never existed, their belongings had never been theirs, and those who didn't respect the obligation to forget had to go else-where, someplace where their memories wouldn't bother anyone. To complete the work, several words that had a more or less ob-vious connection to the slaughter were banned from the language.

181. Are traces of blood not indelible, then, as the proverb has it?

* * *

As she sits, she continues to follow the steps her memories take, daydreaming or dozing, and the day fades away. It's visible in the way the light falls more softly on her face, subtly different from how it fell just a few moments earlier. Not even once does she raise her head to see what's there, farther down the cluttered path where her memory takes her. She couldn't care less. It's too late to worry in what direction her memory might lead her. The slightly anxious but warmhearted young woman to whom you were intro-duced has turned into a marionette made of stone.

In her hands she holds something that's no longer a pen. You lean over her shoulder to get a better look at it, but it's impossible to make out what it is dangling there between her legs, in the folds of the long black skirt she's wearing.

She remembers the surprise she hadn't been able to keep from uttering that day. What Kizito had called his "home" was a room in a house shared by a number of different people—members of his family, friends and friends of friends. She got settled, careful to keep the place sufficiently neat so that it could also serve as her of-fice. There she'd receive people to interview. Since they weren't of-ficially together, Kizito had to constantly refute the suspicion and vouch for the fact that he only saw her by day.

After feeling discouraged for a while, she decided to forget about the Foundation and continue with her project. She would proceed neighborhood by neighborhood and, as with a survey, approach people at random. She would explain her objective to those willing to stop and listen and bring the ones who were prepared to entrust their memories to her back to her room. She'd listen to them without taking any notes so that they wouldn't feel uncomfortable. Once the interview was over, she'd transcribe the story, making sure it did not exceed one page. Such was the procedure she had in mind and initially stuck to.

She began with the area where she was living, around which she drew a perimeter. As soon as she got up in the morning, a wooden plank transformed the bed into a bench, and the table, emptied of everything it had held, became a desk. She opened her computer, which was turned off since she wasn't using it. She always anticipated the crash that might obliterate her work. The only reason for having it there was to give the place an air of professionalism. She took her notes in notebooks that began to pile up fast and to grow into a respectable, encouraging stack.

As soon as she finished an interview, she locked herself in the room long enough to transcribe the account. Then, exhausted, she would either go back to "fish for witnesses," as Kizito called it, or join the rest of the household in their daily routine.

All this time Kizito was going back and forth through the city in his taxi. When he came home they told each other about their day and were surprised at the joy it gave them to come together again, to which he would add what a "shock" it was to see his "little Frenchwoman" looking more beautiful each day. With that expression, well known as it was and probably copied from somewhere, he succeeded in surreptitiously touching something in her. She answered that, if she were really French, he'd make her blush with his praises of which he seemed never to tire.

If you come near her face you will see her weeping. Is it her life that flows down her cheeks, drop by drop? Is it her life that she doesn't even try to hold onto, that gets squeezed into her clothing before it's absorbed there?

TEN

182. When no trace whatsoever was left of the massacres, Niko went right back to work at the forge. Generally speaking, business wasn't as good as it had been before, for lack of customers, but no one complained—especially not Niko, for whom things couldn't be worse, in any case, than when he'd been segregated for the expressions and drawings he engraved on his articles, among other reasons. The others found solace in persuading themselves that having less work wasn't so bad: less water to be drawn from the well, fewer bags to carry for the merchants, fewer people for the mayor to have to listen to, fewer travelers for the taxi driver to transport, and so forth. Niko agreed with this view since, as the workshop was less busy, he had time to finish his articles with greater precision. He spent countless hours fiddling with the curve of a sickle, the roundness of a jug, or the firmness of a handle. On the other hand, for reasons he couldn't explain to himself, he'd stopped engraving expressions or drawings on his products. He now preferred geometric figures, which he invented with unconcealed curiosity and talent. He probably no longer needed to be noticed. The aura he'd acquired during the period that shouldn't be called to mind still surrounded him. Nobody called him Niko the Monkey anymore.

183. Nevertheless, the normality to which Niko tried to adhere was too frail to last. As he knew it to be precarious, he clung to its preservation all the more and, by doing so, weakened it even further.

184. Can a murderer go back to his previous life the way a wanderer puts his sandals back on after removing them to cross a swamp? Does picking up one's regular activities, purging oneself and the outside world from any recollection of the crime committed, allow you to once again become a normal man? Does taking another person's life forbid you to use your own as you see fit?

185. Be that as it may, a long time passed during which Niko had no other concern but his workshop. The only other thing that sometimes preoccupied him was how much he'd fallen behind his contemporaries. All of them were already raising children, while he had never even had a girlfriend. But he avoided thinking about it too much, for the solution wasn't up to him, but rather to the one who, at his birth, had not only been inspired to make him mute but also to give him a smile that made everyone uncomfortable—even the cows (he'd tried repeatedly to smile at them, and they had sped away every time). Mostly he thought of this without any bitterness; he was simply making a resigned observation.

186. One day, when he had just closed the workshop after he was still admiring the objects he'd made that day with satisfaction, he sees a young girl in the distance, carrying one container on her head and another in her hand. Her gait thrusts the image of Hyacinthe at him, the day she was being chased and had passed his forge while he was recovering from the jolt of the pot. That was the day he became a member of the Intentionally Enraged, and . . . "Killed by his son." The phrase surfaces like a mighty deluge. He tries to get rid of it, but instead of vanishing, the four words grow huge inside his head until they occupy it completely. When he manages to turn away from them, it's only to see the faces and hear the screams of his victims. And the phrase returns, "killed by his son," like a finger pointing at him, amplified by the scenes that fuse until they make him feel like he's back in that period, the period he'd done his best to erase. Those eyes. Those bodies. Those screams whose words he didn't know. That blood. The more he denies it, the more it torments him. His father on his knees before him keeps repeating, "See, I told you never to give in to those who have the answers," and he sees himself again, hitting the man on the back of his head with that enormous club that would later crash its weight

onto so many other skulls. The viscous flow of the images drowns his spirit. The woman he'd taken by surprise as she was relieving herself, undoubtedly out of fear. She begged him to let her finish, but he wouldn't hear of it. The two children he told his men to bury alive to punish them for making him run so far. The young woman who threw her baby into the river when she saw he was sending his men after her. The young man whom he'd forced to kill his own parents before slaughtering him, in spite of what he'd promised him through the voice of one of his men. The death of Gaspard in the indifference of a party to celebrate a good day's work.

187. In all the scenes his memory regurgitates, he evolves naturally. He never seems embarrassed by what he thinks, sees, hears, and does. Describing as barbarian people about whom he knew nothing other than that it was the category marked on their identity card. Suppressing the crucial question: "Why?" Why hadn't he asked himself the reason for doing all that? Satisfied to hear them call him "chief." Gulping liters of beer and wolfing down kilos of meat in blind elation amid the dead. Being passionately involved, every morning for months on end, as if it were a ball game. Remaining serene once it was all over. Going back to a normal life after simply removing the bodies. Trampling the blood-oozing ground, lightheartedly, if only in appearance. Spending his time inventing and drawing figures on his objects.

188. Is murder unforgivable because the only person from whom rightful forgiveness could come is no longer there?

189. He also recalls the warning that came to him during the vision he had when he was unconscious. He can't even remember being tempted to keep it in mind and failing to inform the others. That would have allowed him not to add arrogance and a good conscience to cruelty.

190. Suddenly and for the first time Niko felt too small for what he has seen, done, and heard. The emotions, which he's been so good at suppressing, overflowed and spread across the ground in front of him in the form of uncontrollable vomit. The malaise shook him as if it were a question of laying bare to the outside world who, at the very core, he really was. Niko knew what he'd look like exposed this way, and that sickened him even more. He was shaking, too, as if the assurance in which he'd wrapped himself had fallen

off his all too puny shoulders. It left him obscenely naked. His own existence was scrutinizing him with disappointment in its eyes, as if telling him that he was no longer deserving.

191. When he finally collected his wits, he didn't need to think too long before he decided to leave. Being as far away and as alone as possible now seemed urgent, crucial. The world could only inspire unbearable memories in him. So it was mandatory that he withdraw from it.

192. The farthest place he knew of, the only one where he could be alone, was the cave on the island where he'd gone the day he was initiated. He took the cape he wore when leaving the workshop so the outside temperature wouldn't seize him too abruptly. He slid a gourd full of banana juice into a satchel that he attached to the rope he used as a belt, some matches, and, just in case, a roll of thick cord from which he hung objects to be dried. Without even hoping he might use them, he also brought a small bag of sunflower seeds, given to him in exchange for a hoe, which he'd promised himself to plant someday. Finally, out of habit, he grabbed a stick and a machete, essential for making his way to the cave and feeling safe.

193. For a moment he thought of alerting people that he was leaving and saying good-bye. But he realized his absence would certainly not shock anyone. It was all very well and good that he wasn't Niko the Monkey to the villagers anymore, at least not in appearance, but it hadn't made him any less lonely. After a period of time, the forge would be plundered or occupied by someone else, and his traces would be obliterated until they were no more than a memory. He wouldn't be anything anymore. Moreover, if he were to announce his departure, someone might just try to stop him out of politeness, and that he couldn't bear. His need was too pressing. So he left his workshop as usual, as if to go for a walk, and didn't even shut the door. He knew he'd never set foot back there again.

194. A path behind the workshop leads to a road that heads west. It's a narrow, dusty road, crowded morning and evening with people who come and go to work on foot, by bicycle, or by car. Since it was the middle of the day and an uncompromising sun was keeping vagabonds out of sight, he made his way more or less quietly. Only one driver in a van bothered him, suggesting he give him a ride. After a long straight line through the valley, the road

climbed the hill of the Breast of Mukaneza (each hill supposedly represented the breast of a legendary beauty). As he went through the pass there was a small town with a service station in the center that also served as a market and a taxi stand. There fatigue forced him to sit down. For one second he was sorry he hadn't accepted the offer of the van driver, who must have thought he was hitchhiking. At this hour he could have been far away already, maybe even reached the lake. But he couldn't welcome this sort of kindness. His own existence appeared to him as a form of kindness that life was offering him, and he couldn't make himself be open to it any longer. Wasn't it the very sacrifice of this type of kindness, a sign of elementary thoughtfulness, that had launched the blood-spattered eruption of which he'd been one of the most efficient arms? In fact, since kindness leads to behaving toward others the way you'd want them to behave toward you, it's the first thing to be lost when weapons take over. Niko recalls having understood very quickly that it's a matter of annihilating the other as a preventive measure and being guilty of anticipating the evil the other may do to you. Why should he have any right to the kindness he had been the first to trample? Why must he consent to still being alive or picked up for a ride?

195. With these thoughts, new images rushed inside his head, and he couldn't find any subterfuge to lessen their ferocity or keep them at bay. When he was leading the Intentionally Enraged, there was one man whom he respected most, not so much for his work but for the enthusiasm he communicated to the rest of the group. One day, this particular man made an observation as he stopped cutting up a little girl whose skull he'd already smashed and whose severed arm—with which she'd tried to protect herself—he'd dropped. He was amazed that the barbarians' blood spurt forth so precipitously, as if its natural place wasn't to irrigate the body but the earth itself. After a brief initial struggle, the little girl had collapsed and was motionless. Perhaps, he added, we're freeing them from something that's not supposed to be inside them. How could he have seen any humor in those words and ordered his group to laugh? Can he now endure the politeness of others without being strangled by shame? Is it really a matter of kindness? Again nausea overwhelms him and makes him dump everything from the depths of his en-

trails. The faces on which he'd spat before mutilating them. The corpses on which he'd relieved himself as if his whole persona had been reduced to the hatred he felt for the barbarians. The young woman whom he'd asked to be kind to him without being kind to her later on. He'd handed her over to his Intentionally Enraged. The pats on the back he'd been given early in the day for encouragement or at day's end in congratulation. The carefully sharpened machetes. The bodies thrown into ditches, burned, ruined, crushed, dissolved. The return to normal life. The jars calmly drying in the furnace where so many corpses had disappeared. The faces etched by the metal point, thanks to which so many who had tried hiding some of the barbarians had talked. The nights peacefully spent in the same room where he'd humiliated countless captives who would die a few days later, sometimes by his own blows. Inside his head all these visions feed on each other, merging into a piercing white shaft of lightning.

196. When he woke up, it was dark, and he was surrounded by a few lights behind which voices were asking him if he was feeling better. He nodded affirmatively, drank the glass of water they held up to him, made a face that was meant to say thank you, nodded farewell, and went on his way. He had to get far away from everything, from everything that would plunge him back into the time whose memory utters itself in tremors, excretions, and blackouts. He had to get far away, or else, he thought. Having nothing left to throw up he'd soon be spewing blood, brain, and tongue. Only the cave, his isolation, and his obscurity, he thought, could save him from these unbearable thoughts, from the convulsions, the vomiting, and the loss of consciousness that accompanied them as he tried to quicken his step.

197. On the way he should above all not catch sight of the church in which the Intentionally Enraged, with him in the lead, had decimated several hundred people. That bloodbath, by far the most difficult of all the ones he had committed, had definitively established his authority over the group. Yet they'd all boasted about it and been offered several beers and delicious kebabs in reward for the feat. He also needed to watch out for stepping over fallen trees, for outlines that might remind him of Hyacinthe, for individuals who might greet or recognize him, for assailants whose violence

he wouldn't have been able to face. As if that weren't enough, there were the sounds of nature, too, the rumble of water currents, the rustling of the wind in the trees, the cries of animals that could, at any moment, transport him into a nightmare that would shake him up enough to suffer another fainting spell.

198. He pressed on, head down, taking small paths and using the night to make as much progress as he could. Despite his precautions, he still had to stop more than once, stunned by a detail that would unleash bewilderment and uncontrollable convulsions.

199. He reached the lake's shore just before dawn. It didn't take him long to find a boat. Stealing one didn't even bring a shudder to his conscience, tormented by far graver flaws.

200. It was a difficult crossing. He was exhausted, and the rocking of the pirogue, faint as it was, added to his discomfort. During the trip, he tried to take his mind off things by studying the island that was to become his home, shaped so obviously like a nose. The shadows created by the vegetation seemed to outline nostrils, adding to the likeness. Illuminated by the rising sun, the nose that emerged in front of him was enormous. Depending on the angles and the light, it appeared delicate or massive, short or long. A few times Niko was actually amazed to detect some sort of exhalation, but it was just mist, as he later realized. Once he was ashore he didn't bother to fasten the pirogue. He simply pushed it off into the water. Maybe it was his way of making sure that the journey didn't include any return. Or perhaps he meant for that gentle push to send the pirogue back to its rightful owner.

201. A few steps on, a stretch of sand and black rock faced him. Then the forest began, through which he'd have to clear himself a path. Fortunately, he'd brought his machete and a stick, but first he would have to eat something. He dug up two unanticipated sweet potatoes and drank some of his banana juice. The surrounding noises came from little waves, the wind, and animal cries, ibis, crows, or the local *talapoin*, none of which triggered any disastrous memories.

202. At that moment, through the design of the clouds in the bright sky, it seemed his life was glancing at him with a look of severe disapproval. In response, he spent a long time focusing on the sweet potatoes he needed to peel and slowly chew, then on the gourd full of juice, which he drank to the last drop. After this long,

THE PAST AHEAD   95

drawn-out attempt at evasion, his life was still staring at him, and his profound disenchantment seemed to have turned into unfathomable sorrow. Niko could do nothing other than let a seemingly inexhaustible flood of moist beads flow down his cheeks.

203. For the first time in his life his voiceless throat seemed a severe handicap to him. He would have liked to have a voice to really cry out and weep.

204. "Dear reader, if you've been paying attention to the tale, you know what happens next. The climb up the hill, the watch from the top of the tree, the entering of the cave, the fall, the awakening by the guardian angel, the latter's death, Niko's surrender to the group of monkeys, and interspersed between all these moments, his persistent ravings, interrogations, and distractions. On the other hand, you don't know what's happened to him since we left him to examine his previous life. Perhaps that exploration has annihilated the sympathy you may have had for Niko. 'Abandonment and oblivion are the very least of what one might inflict on people like him!' you may try to keep from screaming. Perhaps you're annoyed that you didn't recognize this horror from the start. It may even be possible that you really doubt that the kind and naïve Niko who was dreaming of happiness on the edge of a basin is the same one who killed so many people. To follow Niko, or to hesitate doing so, amounts to wondering whether a murderer is only fully involved in killing at the very instant he commits murder. Or whether his act, once it's been committed, absorbs him completely and definitively. What would you say to someone who insists that even the most relentless murderer merges with his act only at the precise instant that he commits it? Before the act some part of the future assassin is not yet involved in the murder, and afterward, some part of the guilty one can't be figured into it. That is the part that doesn't correspond with the killer and the moral value granted him that might help you decide to stay or not to stay in Niko's company."

205. Is this rift one way of posing the question of forgiveness? Does forgiveness have a limit? If so, what punishment is appropriate for the acts that Niko and so many like him have committed?

*   *   *

It wasn't all that long ago. If she made an effort to recall it, she'd know the exact day and hour, but she'd never taken days and hours very seriously. Not that she didn't notice them or that she forgot—they just seemed like pointless details not worthy of remembrance.

The hotel sent a messenger to her: she had mail, so she hurried over there. Two envelopes, one large, one small. Curious, she opened the first one first.

"Dear Isaro, darling girl." That could only be from her parents. The phrase enveloped her like a tender embrace. "You will never know how much joy, relief, and pride we felt when we received your letter. Your mother and I were deeply moved and, for quite a while, incredulous. We were totally dumbfounded, not because we'd given up hope there would be a sign from you someday, but because we'd yielded so completely to your wishes, which seemed to indicate you didn't want to hear our names uttered ever again. Even now, as my fingers slide across this page, I haven't quite managed to find the assurance and calm of a father addressing his daughter. I feel more as if I'm inside the feverish skin of an adolescent who is writing words he's not convinced he has the right to speak. Your mother isn't sure that the comparison is appropriate, but no matter. It expresses my feelings perfectly and that's all that counts." She smiled at the words in which she recognized her parents the way she'd always known them, each in an incontrovertible role: her father extreme, authoritarian, and affectionate, and her mother expressing the same characteristics but in a less direct manner.

Would she be able to smile if she were there? Probably not. Impossible, actually.

"But we don't want to talk to you about our squabbles. What is important to us above all else is that you do not blame yourself for anything. True, your sudden estrangement made us very unhappy. However, far from holding it against you, we saw it as a sign of a wound that was as grievous as your act was violent. What was the most difficult was your having cut off any access so swiftly. We had to make do with ruminating over our mistakes in our own little corner, frustrated by suddenly finding ourselves against you, but equally concerned with not violating the line you had drawn for us." These words constricted the most sensitive part in her chest and filled her head with thoughts that, in baffling and different ways, represented appeasement, shame, and regret.

"All of this to let you know that there's no need for us to forgive you since you are guilty of nothing. Still, if you need to hear it to feel better, yes, we forgive you. And that's not a concession at all, but it's a joy to see you back in a place that in our eyes you never left." All these convolutions were so like her father that she imagined him, as she imagines him today, sitting solemnly at his desk, her mother standing behind him near the window. In that picture her father forms the phrases, states them out loud, and writes them down if her mother doesn't object, which she often does. He delineates each letter with the greatest of care, even dotting the "j."

"We have taken to heart your reproach that we gave you no explanations. Our undoubtedly debatable idea was not to weigh you down with all that before you were firmly centered in your life. We were afraid of confronting you with a pointlessly burdensome past." She muses without being sure she understands how telling her where she came from could be pointless. "We thought you had already seen more than enough and felt we didn't need to add any further details to that." At this phrase, too, she stopped. How could it be that, during all her time in France, she didn't remember any of the things that had happened, although she'd been old enough to realize what was going on, even if she didn't understand? In fact, she'd always known, but had wanted her parents to tell her what had occurred. In tidying up her memories, that reminiscence revealed a corner that had been left to wither in obscurity and dust. Vague at first, then more and more sharp, she began to see more clearly. After all, what she had held against them was that they hadn't told her what had happened, although she knew.

Spontaneously, the story of the toad and the swallow, which she had tried so hard to recall, was the first thing that came back to her. It was the story her father told her on the plane going to France when she couldn't sleep. Starting with that impression, her memory went back to the moment she was brought to France, which the rest of the letter recounted.

"What happened is that your parents, who were our neighbors for six years, and we were very close friends. We were there to teach French at the International Lycée. Your father was in charge of reception there and your mother was an accountant. Both of them welcomed us into their own family as if we'd always belonged there.

The year the tragedy occurred, we were talking with them about coming with us one day so we could show them our home, too." Memories that came flooding in as forcefully as water fills a lock accompanied these lines.

"Obviously, when the massacres began we hid them in our house, thinking there wouldn't be any risk if they were with foreigners. For a while this was true, but soon the rumors were going around that we were hiding barbarians. I'm not going to explain the meaning of that term to you. It was your father who was the target because your mother, as her identity card showed, had done nothing wrong other than to be his wife." She waited before she went on because she knew what was coming next. And yet she had to read it, the way they'd written it.

"It's as painful for me to tell you the rest as, I imagine, it is for you to read. While we were supposed to be evacuated the following day together with your parents, a team of furious armed youth forced their way into our house. Your father, your mother, your big sister, and you were under a bed. When the leader of the group asked if we were hiding any people I didn't have time to think twice about telling the truth or lying when your mother came out of her hiding place, waving her identity card and begging them not to hurt her husband. The leader asked how many people were under the bed and your mother said there were two persons left: your father and your big sister. They came out, leaving you crouched in the back. Your parents were killed and your sister was taken away. To be sure there was no one left and rather than bending down to look, the leader shot a few bullets through the bed. I won't go into the punishment they had for us, paltry compared to everything else. When they were gone we didn't dare look under the bed, sure they had hit you and dreading to have to find your body. After a long silence, your little voice muttered, 'Mama? Papa?' We couldn't get over the shock of it and took you out. Surely from where you were hiding you'd seen everything." The rest, which she had trouble reading because tears were filling her eyes and the sheet of paper was trembling in her hands, gave her the names of her father, mother, and sister, the address where they used to live, as well as the names of some of their assassins who were none other than people from the area and, in a few cases, friends.

The letter ended with an apology for the ferocity of the account. As long as things were to be told, better tell them once and for all, without trying to omit anything or tone it down. The second envelope contained a card with several folded bills of fifty and a hundred euros. A note said: "In addition to what your father has written, I thought this might be useful to you. I fully support your new life and the completion of your project and I only regret I'm not strong enough anymore to join your effort. Much love, M.-J."

ELEVEN

206. With time Niko is sure he's a kind of prisoner of the monkeys. He must stay where he is, surrounded by them or at least within sight of the one who guards him. His activity is restricted to staying in the cave, following the group when it goes out in search of food, and for the rest of the time being as unobtrusive as possible. If he strays from these rules his guardian grabs his neck as if to strangle him, violently shakes him, and lets out an indeterminate scream, fixing him with a dark look. Then he throws the lifeless skeleton on the ground, staying there to hit him if he tries to get up. Some time later the guard monkey withdraws, a sign that the punishment has come to an end, and Niko can stop inhaling dust, can sit down or stand up again. At the slightest lapse in behavior, punishment comes down on him, brutal and relentless. In the beginning, Niko submits to it, over and over again, but in time he learns to eliminate all that could lead him to be anywhere but at circumspect attention to what's going on around him. Even the nightmares and visions that keep on startling him no longer make him lose control. His eyes, invisible in their sunkenness, let the visions that once undid him file past without betraying any emotion. His empty belly is no longer receptive to the nausea that overcomes him at such moments. Reduced to a motionless shell, his body seems foreign to anything that might stir his mind. He has grown numb to memory.

207. Because they whirl inside his head, memories of the killings are muddled, now forming just a single, similar scene. All the nightmares are one.

208. In his vision he's raking through a papyrus-covered swamp, hoping to find a survivor he can kill. Sometimes he searches for a very long time before he surprises a young man who looks like him and who's singing something to a blood-spattered girl on her knees, resembling Hyacinthe in every aspect. It's always the same couple upon whom he intrudes. He strains his ears to listen to the song the young man murmurs and hears this:

> *When life stops*
> *We go elsewhere.*
> *Some will miss us,*
> *But we're no longer among them.*
> *Others overdo it*
> *And insult the dying.*
> *One less, they rejoice,*
> *Good riddance, and who's next?*
> *They've been dying*
> *For all too long, except for us.*
> *Will it be our turn today?*
> *Will we sleep like the others,*
> *Finally and forever sleep?*
> *If that's the case, my darling,*
> *Close your eyes,*
> *Breathe deeply.*
> *Get ready for your last sigh.*

The boy who so oddly resembles him doesn't look sad as he intones these words. He just seems tired. Tired of running from death.

209. He's barely had time to finish his song and lie down next to his young friend who's dying silently when Niko leaps upon them and hacks them into a thousand pieces. Then, worn out, he sits down on an embankment to catch his breath when his father emerges, holding a spear. Despite the mud that covers him, Niko recognizes who he is.

"It's taken long enough," his father announces calmly, adjusting his spear. "Today it's you who will die."

"No, Father, please forgive me! Have pity on me! Don't kill me!" Niko begs, finding his voice.

"Oh, really, and why shouldn't I kill you? What about you? Did you ever hesitate? I'm not even talking about your cutting me down the way a woodcutter eliminates an unmanageable tree. I'm talking about all the others, including the two over there you just struck down in a way that would terrify even the fiercest animal," his father retorts, clearly impatient to get it over with.

"But it's not my fault. They made me do it. I would never have taken the initiative in any of that!" Niko pleads.

"Quiet!" his father roars furiously. "Did anyone force you to carve up this couple as you just did? If you're so intent on a good reputation, why did you agree to become the leader of the Intentionally Enraged? Why don't you act as if you were at the rear of the column instead of leading the attacks? Why don't you spend the day here, simply sitting? Why don't you go back to the village without having killed anyone, claiming you've decimated dozens? Who would check up on it?"

"It didn't occur to me," Niko stammers before he pulls himself together. "They're watching me. I can't . . ."

"Enough blather!"

Niko sees the point of the spear come at him, straight between his eyes and, instead of blood, vomit spurts from his skull. He wakes up.

210. That's what everything is finally reduced to.

211. Although he's awake, the odor of vomit follows his trail and causes dreadful nausea. So that nothing will penetrate, Niko has made it a habit to close his eyes, lean gently against the wall of the cave, and let himself black out. Sometimes it lasts too long and the guard monkey becomes aware of his absence. Then blows, shaking, and the strangling of his thin neck between the powerful hand of the guard monkey awaken him.

212. On rare occasions he manages to look his fate calmly in the eye and then feels infinitely guilty and ashamed. It makes him wonder what really drove him to flee. Was he trying to escape justice? Punish himself? Is there a punishment that matches his guilt? Is death any solution? And what about isolation? Are the monkeys the executioners of his retribution? Was the mission handed over to them? By whom?

213. He finds it ludicrous to see his situation as a punishment. It's too mild compared to what he has perpetrated, and that leads him back to the beginning of the loop: shame and guilt.

*   *   *

Country, language, and manners came back to her naturally. She found them again rather than discovered them. Besides Kizito, who insists on calling her his "little Frenchwoman," nothing or almost nothing reminds her she ever left this place.

During the trip she took with Kizito she wasn't at all surprised to run into the cows whose long horns on slight bodies give them their characteristic appearance. She instinctively learned the infinite nuances of politeness in language and posture. Without a shudder, she could take a machete in her hands, a tool with many uses: to cut wood for cooking, carve sticks the shepherd uses to control the cattle, help the sower spread the seed, and cut anything and everything for the butcher. She's even seen children use it as a ruler when drawing geometric figures in their notebooks and people place it between two supports to be used as a bench. With the same effort as everyone else, she has managed to mask the other use it can have.

She didn't want to return to the place where she had escaped from death. Her pretext was that she had no time and that the distance was too great, but when Kizito insisted on wanting to take her there, she had to confess she was afraid. What would she have done if, upon arriving at the house of which her memory had such a radiant picture, she found its ruins overgrown with vegetation? Would she have been able to endure the void that nature used to cover her family and the trace of their sacrifice? How would she have reacted if she'd found other children, a happy, smiling family in the courtyard where she remembers she learned to walk? Without being ripped apart by sorrow and turmoil, would she have accepted that new flowers are now growing on the land where she had seen her family's blood flow, where she floundered around to get away? Would she have resisted the hatred and despair that seized her? What would she have done with it? Unless he had a straight answer to these innumerable questions, Kizito understood that it was better to avoid going back there. Tactfully, he didn't bring it up again.

They did so many things during that journey to which she thinks back in disbelief today. How did they ever manage to get to know so many people and, thanks to these encounters, listen to so many stories, climb to the summit of volcanoes to see the gorillas, tour the Island du Nez, learn to make baskets and pottery, milk goats, and so much more?

Of everything she saw, did, and heard, she remembers the meeting with the gorillas above all. Because he had so little faith in the two guides, Kizito finally decided to follow her. After two days of climbing through a tangled, humid forest they'd come upon a group of the large apes, fascinating because of their size, but more so because of their eyes. While the four of them were squatting a few steps away from the group, she was overcome when in their gaze she saw none of the brutality or the facetiousness for which movies had prepared her—for a gorilla's eyes are not the vacant eyes of a trout or a cow, nor were there any of the bottomless interrogations that are reflected in human eyes. She wondered if gorillas feel any scorn, resentment, or hatred among themselves or toward other monkeys or animals. If not, could they be driven in that direction? Seeing she was being observed by those powerful eyes, she pondered the likelihood of gorillas having their own commentary on humans. On the trek back, she'd asked the guide these things, which he jotted down in a notebook. He collected the questions travelers posed after a visit, he told her.

During that same trip Kizito's mother had shown her how banana wine is made, and then she learned to make it herself. Since her teacher asked her to put the lesson into practice, she thought of adding sugarcane juice to the mix to increase the sweetness and alcohol level. She also filtered the mixture much more than was generally done and came up with a liquor everyone loved.

Thanks to this discovery, she's now able to contribute to the household expenses and her project's needs. She decided to sell her beverage on market days, side by side with the vendors of banana juice and sorghum beer. She soon acquired a large clientele and was able to recruit a saleswoman so she could devote her time to producing the drink itself. Better yet, a little while ago, a man, who introduced himself as the head of an important brewery, proposed that they develop her invention together and produce the drink on a larger scale. She didn't respond to him right away and for a long time was satisfied to play with the irony of fate that had led her to commerce and its techniques, over which she had suffered so in her studies. She wondered, too, whether she could really become involved in the sale of alcohol, whose excesses she'd always abhorred. To which Kizito, always ready with an answer to all her questions and a solution to all her doubts, replied that in this country, anyway, people couldn't go on living without being in a state of intoxication at all times. The best way to be of use to them was to provide them with anything that could help them escape. Drinking helped them avoid thinking of what they needed to forget so they wouldn't go mad and be unable to tolerate life among the others. That notion made a big impression on her, but at the time, she was content to simply comment that he was talking like a French Romantic poet whose name she couldn't remember. Baudelaire, perhaps. She never showed it when something stirred her brain too much. Routinely, she preferred keeping her thoughts to herself, and that included thoughts the outside world provoked in her. His mouth pursed, presumably like a Frenchman's, or so he thought, Kizito had replied, "But I am a romantic, too!"

During the time when she had not yet responded to the brewery manager, she was dreaming of everything that the money would allow her to do. Kizito didn't understand why she didn't grab the opportunity. How could she let someone so important wait? He promised her that as soon as she accepted the brewery offer he would either sell his taxi or keep it, depending on what would be best for the project, and then he would assist her. He didn't hide the fact that part of his reason was to stay close to her, for he thought that at times she was surrounded by other people a little too much.

She knew she wasn't going to accept the offer. It came too close to a conventional way of dealing with life, something she couldn't allow herself to do. It was the same reasoning that kept her from accepting Kizito's marriage proposal, a desire he'd manifested since the beginning. Perhaps it was also the reason she'd refused to see her parents all those years and she vanished the moment they arrived. Nothing else seemed right to her. The only things that were right, it was blindingly obvious, was living on the fringes, suffering, and death. She never did more than tolerate the rest.

Once in a while, more and more rarely, she thinks of the other one, no longer remembering what it was they had together. When with some effort she does recall it, she doesn't understand.

TWELVE

214. Reduced to the most extreme acquiescence, Niko still managed to preserve one uncontrollable part of himself. In his nook, everything he was except for his physical body was blooming.

215. Far from this resilient bit of ground, where darkness covered him, Niko stared at the three people who arrived at the cave's entrance one at a time, saw the ragged mummy, and, shrieking loudly, turned away from it.

216. The first one was Uwitonze, his now aged schoolteacher. Obviously spent, stooped over his cane, he'd waited to raise his head until he was right in front of the cave. Then when his eyes crossed the dark eyes of the monkey's corpse, he wielded his cane as if to defend himself against the specter. It was the middle of the day and, sweating as much from the effort as from fear, he withdrew without lowering his cane, muttering something at the threat. Once he'd gained a little distance, he knelt down, undoubtedly to ask forgiveness for almost having blasphemed by crossing the entrance.

217. From the garden, where Niko was subservient to no one, he was happy to imagine the old man also caught in the web of memory, since he apparently felt the need to seek refuge here. The monkey's ghost must have reminded him of the risk that anyone ran who broke the taboo of entering the cave, which he must have been told at least once, on the day he became a man. There, in front of the cave, Uwitonze must have been afraid to be sucked in, and so he backed away.

218. What memories could Uwitonze possibly be fleeing from? Not a single one, from what Niko had been able to see and hear. Protected by his advancing age and by the position that people had always known him to have, to which anyone who'd been in his class could attest, he had refused to get mixed up with the killings. In the beginning, he even came to preach to those who were involved, begging them to please listen to their old teacher and stop massacring innocent people. All he could see in the goings-on was an absurd tragedy where former students were hurling themselves at one another. When killing grew into a habit, his own efforts notwithstanding, he stopped shouting his disapproval, understanding that from now on the death-obsessed ears would no longer forgive him. Thereafter he tried to reason with people only in private, but to no avail.

219. In reality, Uwitonze hadn't stayed completely aloof from what was going on. He'd lent a hand to those who'd pushed some into death's bottomless hole. Indeed, because he had been critical of everyone, they suspected him of hiding people at his house. A gang was formed to check on him. When he saw them coming, he took the leader aside, offered him money, whereupon they left. But soon the rumor started up again. "Uwitonze is protecting a nest full of barbarians!" they insisted. So another group came to see him. Like the first time, by using money and because of his status, which a search would not have left unscathed, Uwitonze managed to avoid an inspection of his house so that the fifteen people who were in hiding there were not discovered. Sensing that he couldn't be evasive indefinitely and knowing what would be the end result, Uwitonze asked his charges to leave. Their lives as well as his own were in danger. He said a long prayer with them before relinquishing them to the night. His wife gave them something to live off for a few days—bananas, water, juice, bread, and sugar—in a sturdy bag. The next night, the celebration that marked the end of the workday was held in an exceptionally joyful mood. The day had started with the slaughter of fifteen barbarians, and the rest of the work hadn't been substandard either.

220. He'd understood. Clustered together in fear, his forsaken group hadn't been able to abide by his instructions that each of them head in a different direction. He didn't go to the place where

they'd been murdered, afraid that an uncontrollable reaction would betray the fact he knew the victims. He stayed home where the scene of their death came to keep him company. Those who boasted they'd been their executioners sketched it out in detail, and his own imagination finally burned a picture into his mind that wouldn't ever leave him. Uwitonze wept every time he visualized the scene, but he remained dignified while his tears flowed inwardly. There, the mixture of his sobs and the sinister image produced a sour mash that ate away at everything that until then had allowed him to prevail. Vanquished, he soon was unable to stand up without his cane. He knew that, after his skeleton, his dignity would be affected. It was to avoid a display of this defeat in the eyes of everyone, both those who mattered and the others, that he had retreated to this place.

221. That, in any case, is the explanation Niko has chosen to provide.

222. What does it do for him to recall or imagine these stories?

223. With Uwera things were different. He merely heard her shriek. She didn't come close enough for him to see her in the doorway. She moved away, uttering a cry just like the one that would lead you to her in the middle of the marketplace, where for years she was the best-known vendor of banana wine. It's by that cry that he recognized her.

224. Like everyone else, Niko knew what had happened to Uwera. Widowed by what is unfit to be mentioned in passing, she subsequently became pregnant. With unrelenting spite, everyone had wondered at the miracle that honored the village with a second known case of Immaculate Conception. Some had even gone so far as to ask her what she'd done to deserve such grace. In reality, they all knew, or could well imagine, how she'd become pregnant.

225. The minuscule child that came out of her belly seemed hesitant. After a brief life, which essentially was no more than one long death struggle, he made his choice and died.

226. The entourage she always flaunted, except when she needed to attract customers in the hubbub of the market, didn't survive this event. More and more frequently, Uwera was possessed by an unpredictable, violent need to shout, run, and lash out. When the urge let go of her, she'd collapse in such over-exhaustion it made

her look like a wreckage. When at last she'd come to, she apologized to all those whom she had physically abused, wash up, and groom herself, only to wait for the next breakdown.

227. Throughout the time he was trying to pick up the strands of a normal life, Niko had always stayed away from the young woman. Every time he saw her, his brain would form itself into an anguished question mark. He was sure that what was happening to Uwera wasn't all that foreign to him but didn't have the strength to give it any serious thought. Could she have been one of the manifold companions of whom he'd taken advantage at an unspeakable epoch?

228. Had she come here on her own, or had they forced her just to be rid of her?

229. Shortly after Uwera, Shema arrived. Moving forward on all fours, a position that might indicate exhaustion as well as deference or even piety, he presented himself in front of the entrance to the cave. Niko watched him prostrate himself before the specter of the monkey and sprinkle it with water. Shema seemed not in the least amazed by this discovery, which had so horrified his predecessors. Niko was afraid the man would come in and find him there. The monkeys, crouching in the same shadows as he, seemed to share his apprehension. They uttered cries that undoubtedly were meant to chase the intruder away. Shema understood and went back the way he had come.

230. Niko knew Shema as well, a storyteller whose tales had educated his daydream world as well as his reality. He connected him especially to a story that had something to do with a toad and a swallow, the former being ugly, huge and fat as he would repeat incessantly, and the second beautiful, nimble, and brazen. He remembered that the two of them had made a bet to be the first to reach the end of the world. First the crafty toad asks his peers to help him win the challenge by answering the swallow's call when she'd pass overhead. As the race begins, all the toad does is submerge himself in the water and resurface a few moments later. The swallow, on the other hand, disappears swift as an arrow. As agreed, every time she flies over a swamp she comes down lower and twitters, "Toad, are you there?" and hears a croak: "Go faster, my beauty, I've been waiting for you." Flying over peaks and valleys, the swallow can't manage to get ahead of the toad, who waits for her every-

where, all the way to the edge of the world. Finally, before she dies of exhaustion, she acknowledges that she has lost the bet. And the tale draws the conclusion that, if you want to succeed, strength is worth less than allies.

231. Unable to be satisfied with imagining animals onstage, Niko had created other versions. In one of these settings, the swallow cheats as well by having friendly swallows take the relay. After pretending to fly off, she comes back to the point of departure, where she finds the toad sitting quietly. The two rivals understand they're on the same wavelength and burst out laughing. In another of his versions, the swallow and the toad find each other upon arrival and taunt each other, each thinking it's the other one who's been had. At last, they understand they're merely the final runners in a relay race without a winner, and they go off in a huff.

232. Niko thinks he knows what brings Shema to seek refuge here. In fact, since the end of the unmentionable events, Shema was the only one not allowed to pick up his customary activities again—that is to say, to tell stories. They didn't want to hear his tales for fear, undoubtedly, that he might raise something better left unspoken. To make sure he wouldn't disobey the imposed silence, they locked him up in a house at some distance from the village from which his cries and moans couldn't be heard. They brought him the food he needed to survive, and every now and then someone changed his bedding. But it was merely an apparent silence, because internally he had a permanent gathering that listened to old stories and especially to his new ones. In the latter, it was above all a matter of what no one wanted to hear.

233. How did Shema manage to escape?

234. The parade in front of the cave resulted in Niko no longer being the center of the monkeys' attention. He took advantage of that to crawl to the entrance unseen, into a slightly higher recess from where he could watch Uwitonze, Uwera, and Shema, companions in thought or creations of his imagination.

*   *   *

Long before the Foundation abandoned her, she realized that making her interviews in the prisons happen was an impossible challenge. Even for the families, visits are limited to a few minutes a week. At first, the procedure had seemed like a joke to her. On visiting day the prisoners come out in groups of fifty. They can be recognized by their pink uniforms. They line up against the wall. Those visitors who are admitted inside stand about twenty meters away, facing them, also in a line. When the signal is given, they take a few steps forward to put down in the center whatever they brought for the prisoners. At the second signal, they draw back at the same time that the detainees move forward to pick up their packages. It's then that arguments often break out because, even though the packages are marked, they don't always end up in the right hands. At the third signal the most astonishing thing happens: words that quickly grow into a shapeless cacophony fly back and forth between the two lines. Family news, recommendations, legal questions, insults, or laughter come and go from visitors to prisoners and back again. At the fourth whistle blow, which always comes too soon and well before the projected ten minutes, or so it seems to everyone who protests, the visit is over. The prisoners, a gun trained on them from the onset by guards on the ground and high above, go back in, and the families leave. The scene is repeated from morning to night as many times as necessary to let every person in the building pass through.

The first time she was present at these visits was by accident. It was not long after her arrival, and she was trying to meet the prison director. While she was waiting for an answer to her request for an interview, the visit began. She came back several times and, for lack of any answer, she attended the scene whose absurdity with time began to be colored by unbearable cruelty and despair. She stopped attending the visits when she stopped waiting for a response, and that was the day she decided to do the interviews at Kizito's house.

It's hard to comprehend the effect the interviews have on her. Their transcripts fill the cardboard boxes piled up in a corner of the room.

At first she devoted herself to it with the pleasure of someone who sees a cherished project become real. She wanted to see it as a new departure from a better-controlled destiny, in keeping with her new emancipation from what had made her so unhappy for so many years. Of course, the venture didn't begin the way she'd expected it to, but it had never seemed that the essence of it was called into question because of the Foundation's withdrawal. Once decided, she started her work in the street. After the first week, she settled on four interviews a day. Stated that way, it seems insignificant, but it actually took her all day. Finding an available person, explaining the plan, gaining trust, listening, posing questions, and transcribing what had been said took two or three hours per interview. It became clear quickly enough that a day wasn't sufficient to write up the definitive form of the stories she derived from a report. Thus, Isaro spent more and more of her nights working, and when she'd finish, instead of sleeping, she reread her earlier writing. Two or three times Kizito surprised her, and in the way he had of trying to be humorous, he'd compare her to a phantom.

To anyone watching her closely, it was obvious that the task was beginning to consume her. The memories of others, whose guardian she became, didn't just enter her ears and leave through her arm and pen in the form of ink. Just as urine isn't the banana beer imbibed a few hours earlier, what she wrote was different from what she had seen and heard. The contrast between the two stayed within her and, more and more conspicuously, transformed and ate away at her.

"Where has my little Frenchwoman gone?" Kizito asked her one day, covering his question with a lighthearted tone. While she granted him a smile, intending to let him know she was really there, she knew what he meant: where was the enthusiastic girl she was when she arrived, during the marvelous trip they'd taken together, and some time before that? Why was she inflicting work upon herself that was so clearly beginning to asphyxiate her? Did she see how he suffered from the trivial role to which she had reduced him? She grasped the questions Kizito had carefully abridged into a single one so well that, from that day on, she no longer dared face him—or anyone else, for that matter. She locked herself in her room.

At first, Kizito and the others pretended to interpret it as mere sulking. They will change their minds, perhaps, when they hear something fall in the room, and when that heavy sound is followed by a silence too long and too perfect for it not to worry them.

That is the moment it arrived, barely visible in the half-light of the room.

THIRTEEN

235. Niko realized that Uwitonze, Uwera, and Shema had come here only to wait for death. Nothing they do links them to life. They're lying down most of the time, and at dusk they go out. That is all they do.

236. As if they'd agreed on it beforehand, the three of them have built their shelters side by side. They've made horizontal excavations in the ground, covered them with foliage and stones against the rain. From where Niko can see them, the little earthen hillocks look like ill-protected graves.

237. They stay put all day long, and only when the sun has vanished completely below the horizon do they all come out to sit at the entrance to their holes, facing the eastern constellations. That's how, in silence, they keep watch until fatigue or weariness overcomes them and they crawl back into their hole.

238. Niko feels he lives with them and so considers the three earthen hillocks as a village of which he is a virtual inhabitant. His fear of the monkeys and his frailty don't allow him to actually join them and dig a fourth lair beside the other three, as he would like to do. In his mind he has named the village: Iwacu, which means *at home*. He enjoys thinking that his idea has taken flight and reached them and that they, too, think of it in those terms. That way, both the image and the name would be the secret link between them.

239. He shares something else with them as well: resignation. Lately he's been letting himself slip into it with a certain joy. He's even surprised himself recently when he noticed that his mind,

once incessantly agitated by uncontrollable fantasy, is no longer struggling, has been extinguished, like a flame that darkness has defeated. The void is taking over. He no longer lays himself open to the memories that so violently obsessed him only a short while ago.
240. To endure. Nothing motivates him except a subtle warmth, a dying indication of a life perhaps already gone.
241. His outsider's eye can clearly see that soon it's only Uwera and Shema who watch at night, barricading the entrance to Uwitonze's lair. Not long thereafter Shema is alone, using his last strength to block Uwera's hole. When it's Shema's turn, Niko is sorry he can't go over to close up his hole.
242. Is it the odor of their corpses he smells or his own?
243. Are the monkeys still paying any attention to him? Why did they deal with him this way? Is it a mission? Who is behind it? In any event, he perceives that gladness is returning to the group of monkeys. Is it because they've finished mourning, because they no longer have to keep an eye on their prisoner? Is it because the three troublemakers aren't there anymore? Is it because of the good weather, which makes the colors of nature come out of their recesses and the other animals out of their silence, that they're in such a good mood?
244. Impervious to the racket the monkeys make, Niko is seized by an assault he doesn't fight. In his body, under attack from insects, his life is gradually yielding ground. First it leaves the hands and feet, but very quickly it must retreat from every limb. Perhaps it thinks that the insects will make do with this area alone long enough for his life to regain strength and retaliate. But that doesn't take their appetite into account, which commands them to cover the body's entire surface, forcing Niko's life to shrink back inward. Once there, it doesn't wait long to hand the belly over to bad smells and put up its last bastion in the chest and head. A heart. A head. Niko is flooded with suffocating pain.
245. Is it he who spreads through the air in the form of an unbearable smell and in the ground as a viscous, blackish liquid that the sickened insects leave for the worms?
246. In a delicate, almost imperceptible movement, his heart persists in its routine. Just as slowly, his brain, overtaken by pain, contains a single query: what will come next?

247. Niko doesn't feel he has the right to think of paradise, reserved for people whose counter-example he realizes he is, and for goats. So at one moment he sees death as the brutal end point after which he will be nothing. But the picture of being entirely reduced to such a radical negation terrifies him. He reaches the point where he thinks that the hell of birds, which he visited in his dream, wouldn't be such a terrible compromise. But being punished eternally for not having known how to use a life he hadn't wished for seems equally unbearable to him.

248. Impasse and pain. Fortunately, he dies.

249. Is it the monkeys' laughter that accompanies his last breath? Or maybe it's the demons he chose to join that welcome him?

250. Niko's life surrenders its final stronghold. It leaves him to face what he'd been dreading and what the insects, worms, and humidity are focusing on making real as they meticulously eat away at, dissolve, and evaporate his flesh, his organs, and his bones.

251. Nothing.

*　*　*

Together with the mail she received, she's left the rough drafts of all her letters on her desk. The last one is illegible, covered with deletions. You get the feeling that she tried to say something that won't come and that, in the end, every phrase is beside the point, is beyond words. This is perhaps more obvious in the draft than in this transcription:

"Dear parents,

I am incapable of telling you what I really felt as I read your letter. I think it was a mixture of relief and regret. I was relieved to know at last and overwhelmed once again by the awareness of how unfair I have been by ascribing bad intentions to you when all there ever was was love.

Strangely enough, I wasn't shocked by what you told me about the fate of my parents. That lay buried deep inside me somewhere, and in a way, I knew it all along. I read it as the confirmation that allows me to accept it and move on to something else.

When I speak of accepting this event, I believe it's an exaggeration. Let's say that I'm trying to live with it instead of against it.

Sometimes when I pass a man in the street, for one reason or another I wonder if that isn't the one who killed them—a sign that I'm not letting go of it. "What if that's him?" That question arises for me more and more frequently as the symbol of an unchanging past. Similarly, some young girls make me think of my sister, who may have survived. Even the slightest demeanor, gesture, or expression is enough to thrust me into this unease. At such moments I feel trapped, forbidden to move forward or go back. But they're merely parentheses in my life, which is otherwise happy.

When I spoke to you of moving on to something totally different, I meant that I feel very differently disposed than a while ago. I really want to see you! And that's an urgent desire, as if I'm driven by the whole period that I went astray. I would like to see you. What would you say if I invited you to take the next plane to come and see me? If you are unable to do that, I will do it myself. And I won't come alone. It's funny but I really feel that it's urgent, although after so many years you might think a few days or weeks more wouldn't matter so much.

You're not dreaming, it really is a hint I gave you just above. I won't say anything else about it so you won't start getting any ideas instead of appreciating it for yourselves.

The news is that I've also started writing a small text. I'll let you read it as soon as I've put all the drafts together into a legible whole, which at present are scattered across my room. I'll tell you right now that the story of Niko (the character's name) is anything but simple and comforting. When I began I didn't really think about it in those terms but I realize that, depicted in this way, he's a bit like the one who may have done what it is I've tried to come within reach of, to understand—killing and forgiving.

As for the rest, my project, which almost came to a halt after the Foundation dropped it, seems to be having a rebirth. Unexpected perspectives are opening up at the same time that I'm discovering new talents in myself: you have to get used to the idea that your daughter isn't merely a hardened adventuress, a seasoned interviewer, but also a fine businesswoman! I'll tell you more in person, very soon I hope.

Lovingly,
Your Isaro"

As a postscript she added that she was ultimately sending it as a fax, because she was too impatient to wait for the mail to deliver her letter. She gave the number at the hotel where a reply could be sent.

All this had been rewritten dozens of times. Did she write and rewrite it to hide, or to identify, her true feelings at that moment? Is it possible that she was happy at the time and then became fiercely distraught shortly thereafter?

When she returned from sending the fax, she ran into Kizito as he was coming home from work. At his suggestion, she finally decided to call her parents. The way she kept wasting time while she was prepared to live with them normally again seemed foolish to him. Why not phone them, talk to them, and hear them? Perhaps . . . Unconvinced, she accepted and followed his advice. He couldn't understand.

As they were walking along, trying to find a telephone booth, she looked at Kizito, wanting to tell him she loved him. Instead of that, a bewildering question exploded in her head: "What if it was he?"

That same evening, when she returned from the phone call that hadn't done her as much good as she'd hoped, Kizito asked her where she'd been.

252. "Dear friend, this story belongs to you now. If it interested you, read it again one day, being careful not to become too absorbed by the play of the narrative, for what's essential lies elsewhere. If it seemed clumsy to you, tell it to others, but improve upon what I may have phrased badly. Finally, if it moved you, rest assured that you ought not to take it for anything other than an unintended lie, a remedy that doesn't work.

Isaro Gervais,
One rainy day."

*   *   *

She is sitting in the same position, motionless, holding the thing that is impossible to identify. She moves, and the shimmer between her legs makes you think she's holding a knife. She gets up. She goes over to her desk and rereads the final words of the story she'd clung to the past few days as if it were a lifeline. The name Niko, which she glances at here and there, barely means anything to her, although it is the fruit of her own imagination and she's taken immense pains to bring him to life.

She flips through the pages without paying any real attention. They seem foreign to her. She's sure she'll never read them again. Already she isn't there any longer.

Did she darken these pages with only what she wanted to put behind her so as not to see it anymore? Did she leave on them what she no longer is, thus declaring who it is she would like to be? Or else did she make the effort only to convert at least one unknown person into a friend and offer him this in memory of herself?

You know what she's going to do, but you stay in the shadows from which you've been watching her since the beginning.

Before she closes her eyes, she checks to make sure nothing in front of her will prevent her fall. As her eyelids lower over her eyes, her smile unfolds, cold and silent.

The instant that she lets herself topple forward, tightly holding the thick wooden handle, does she think of the diving she liked to do in the public swimming pool when she was little? What does she say to herself in that interminable second while she must be fighting her reflexes as she falls, to keep herself straight and not let go of the dagger pointed at her heart?

The End

GILBERT GATORE
was born in Rwanda in 1981. Forced to flee his country with his
family in 1994, he found refuge in what was then Zaire and came
to France in 1997. During the civil war, he kept a diary that was
later lost during his escape. In an attempt to re-create what he had
written, he started to write *The Past Ahead*. He is a graduate of the
Department of Political Science in Lille and of the HEC (École des
Hautes Études Commerciales) in Paris and is a two-time winner
of the University Short Story Prize. *The Past Ahead,* his first novel,
was short-listed for the Prix Goncourt du Premier Roman in France
and won the Ouest-France Prize in 2008. This novel is volume one
of *Figures de la vie impossible.*

Born in Indonesia and raised in the Netherlands, MARJOLIJN
DE JAGER has been living in the United States since 1958. After
a forty-year career teaching French language and literature, during which she worked as a part-time literary translator, she now
translates full-time (since 1999), both from French and Dutch, with
a special focus on Francophone African literature. Her numerous
literary prizes include an NEA Translation Grant (2005) and the
Distinguished Member Award from the African Literature Asso-
ciation (2011). She lives in Connecticut with her husband and three
cats. Her website is mdejager.com.

About *The Clinic*

Faith Wells, M.D., a brilliant cardiologist, realizes an opportunity to set her wealthy male patients up for a different kind of appointment, one outside of the doctor's office. This ultimately leads to Faith creating a high-class escort service, using her medical expertise to provide a heart-safe experience.

To learn more about the *Secret Lives of Moms* series, visit the author's website at michelleleenovels.com.